A Sillitoe Selection

Longman Imprint Books
General Editor: Michael Marland CBE

A selection from the series

There is a Happy Land Keith Waterhouse
Nine African Stories Doris Lessing
The Experience of Colour *edited by* Michael Marland
***The Human Element and other stories** Stan Barstow
***The Leaping Lad and other stories** Sid Chaplin
Conflicting Generations Five television scripts
***A Sillitoe Selection** *edited by* Michael Marland
***Late Night on Watling Street and other stories** Bill Naughton
Black Boy Richard Wright
The Millstone Margaret Drabble
Fair Stood and Wind for France H.E. Bates
Scene Scripts Seven television plays
The Experience of Work *edited by* Michael Marland
Breaking Away *edited by* Marilyn Davies *and* Michael Marland
A Hemingway Selection *edited by* Dennis Pepper
Friends and Families *edited by* Eileen *and* Michael Marland
Ten Western Stories *edited by* C.E.J. Smith
The Good Corn and other stories H.E. Bates
The Experience of Sport *edited by* John L. Foster
***Loves, Hopes, and Fears** *edited by* Michael Marland
The African Queen C.S. Forester
***A Casual Acquaintance and other stories** Stan Barstow
Eight American Stories *edited by* D.L. James
Cider with Roise Laurie Lee
The L-Shaped Room Lynne Reid Banks
The Pressures of Life Four television plays
The Experience of Prison *edited by* David Ball
Saturday Night and Sunday Morning Alan Sillitoe
***A John Wain Selection** *edited by* Geoffrey Halson
Jack Schaefer and the American West *edited by* C.E.J. Smith
Goalkeepers are Crazy Brian Glanville
A James Joyce Selection *edited by* Richard Adams
Cut of the Air Five radio plays, *edited by* Alfred Bradley
Could It Be? *edited by* Michael Marland
The Minority Experience *edited by* Michael Marland *and* Sarah Ray
Scene Scripts Two Five television plays
Caribbean Stories *edited by* Michael Marland
An Isherwood Selection *edited by* Geoffrey Halson
A Thomas Hardy Selection *edited by* Geoffrey Halson
While They Fought *edited by* Michael Marland *and* Robin Willcox
The Wave and other stories Liam O'Flaherty
Irish Short Stories *edited by* Frances Crowe
The Experience of Parenthood *edited by* Chris Buckton
The Experience of Love *edited by* Michael Marland
Twelve War Stories *edited by* John L. Foster
The Birds and other stories Daphne du Maurier
A Roald Dahl Selection *edited by* Roy Blatchford
A.D.H. Lawrence Selection *edited by* Geoffrey Halson
I'm the King of the Castle Susan Hill
Sliding Leslie Norris

*Cassette available

LONGMAN IMPRINT BOOKS

A Sillitoe Selection

Eight short stories by Alan Sillitoe

selected and edited by Michael Marland
with a specially written introduction by the author

Longman

LONGMAN GROUP LIMITED
Longman House,
Burnt Mill, Harlow, Essex

*This Edition is published by arrangement with W.H. Allen and Co.
The Stories first appeared in their volumes*
The Loneliness of the Long-Distance Runner and
The Ragman's Daughter

First published 1968
Twelfth impression 1981

ISBN 0 582 23373 9

Printed in Hong Kong by
Yu Luen Offset Printing Factory Ltd

Contents

A compact cassette recording of *The Bike* and *On Saturday Afternoon* read by Alan Sillitoe is also available from the publishers.

Acknowledgements

We are grateful to W. H. Allen & Co for permission to reproduce copyright material from *Saturday Night and Sunday Morning, Loneliness of the Long Distance Runner* and *Key to the Door* by Alan Sillitoe.

Photograph Acknowledgements

The sequence of photographs at the end of the book was taken by Andrew Whittuck. Photographs on p. 168 appear by permission of the British Broadcasting Corporation (below) and Rediffusion, London (above).

To the Student Reader

The trouble with the title "short stories" for labelling the sort of writing that is in this collection is that it puts so much emphasis on *story*. And the word "story" usually brings clear expectations to the reader's mind: happenings, adventures, the excitement of events, a definite sorting-out kind of ending, and a story-thread of "what happens next?" dragging the reader breathlessly on. This is what "story" has come to mean in most people's minds from their experience of comics, popular films, and television serials. But it's not quite right for the "short stories" of this collection, or, for that matter, of those by other authors.

Labels don't much matter, we may rightly feel, but they can have one bad effect: if we expect one thing and unexpectedly find another, our disappointment may hamper our enjoyment. However good the custard pie, it won't taste good to our palates if we bite it expecting cheese. And if you bite into these stories hoping to find the taste of the detective "story" or the adventure "story", you'll miss their true flavour.

What then should you expect? I'd say first and foremost: people. People, of course, come into all story-telling, but often only so that the author can arrange the events, for events need people. In these stories by Alan Sillitoe, the people, the characters, are the main interest. Each of us in our lives meets a bewildering variety of people. Usually they pass us by. Sometimes we think about them, but frequently only as far as they affect *us*. More rarely, but perhaps more interestingly, we wonder about *them*, their lives, their circumstances, even their *feelings*. And this is the starting point of most of these (and in fact most really good) stories: a sympathetic curiosity about what makes people tick, and then an imaginative attempt to show it, invent it if necessary, in a story.

□ There are, of course, "happenings" in these stories:

□ a serious fire is started in *The Firebug*;

a woman leaves her husband and later is run over in *The Fishing-boat Picture*;

□ a man hangs himself in *On Saturday Afternoon*;

□ a boy is wrongly accused of stealing in *The Bike*.

Yet the real "adventures" of these stories lie in the changes in the reader's mind: the gradual growth of understanding, and the sympathetic involvement with the characters. In fact, you'll find many of the "big events" happen only on the sidelines, as it were, as if the author is not especially interested in these events for their own sake. There is an arrest in *The Ragman's Daughter*, for instance, but it is described in five lines. Or in *The Fishing-Boat Picture*, it is not the *death* that is made into the climax, but the man's *thoughts* later. The effort and detail which an "adventure" writer would put into these moments is put by Alan Sillitoe into letting us know the state of mind and the emotions of the main characters.

Among these main characters the reader needs to include the story-teller in those stories which are told by an "I". The "story-teller" is not "the author", but a character invented by the author, with a way of speaking and ideas and emotions to suit that character.

In some ways short stories like these are nearer to poems than to full-length novels. Probably if you come to them expecting simply very short novels you'll by disappointed. In a novel we live with the main character for a long time; follow him through a series of incidents; see him in a web of other characters' lives, and watch him slowly unfold and change. So the art of the novel is to some extent the art of sequence and development. On the other hand, the art of these stories is very largely the art of the significant moment. The author has made a sudden swoop into the lives of each of his characters and brought out for us a few moments that matter, moments which the author convinces us are ones which really show the essence of that character.

At first one may think of the people of these stories as a gallery of oddities. Certainly the characters are not "average", "respectable" people: Frankie Buller is mentally retarded; Ernest is a victim of shell-shock, a broken down boozer; the man in *On Saturday Afternoon* would be called a manic depressive; Tony, in *The Ragman's Daughter*, is totally without morals and lives only for kicks and sex; Colin, in *The Bike*, is likeable in many ways, but has a rebellious grudge against society. "Surely," the reader may ask, "the author's deliberately choosing to write about very unrepresentative people." There is no real way of explaining why an author chooses to write about *these* and not *those* characters; the nearest explanation is that given by Alan Sillitoe, in his introduction on page 125, when he writes of:

> the misty and occasionally musty vision of a face whose features are involved in some form of emotion, suffering in particular circumstances that force me to the act of recording them.

Sometimes you will think that the "suffering" is all of the character's own making; at other times you might feel the character is a "creature of circumstance" caught by forces which he cannot escape. But in all the stories you will surely feel a sympathy for the character, likeable or unpleasant, full of himself or pathetic, which comes not from judging but from recognising with the author the living features of humanity.

MM

The Bike

The Easter I was fifteen I sat at the table for supper and Mam said to me: "I'm glad you've left school. Now you can go to work."

"I don't want to go to wok," I said in a big voice.

"Well, you've got to," she said. "I can't afford to keep a pit-prop like yo' on nowt."

I sulked, pushed my toasted cheese away as if it was the worst kind of slop. "I thought I could have a break before starting."

"Well you thought wrong. You'll be out of harm's way at work." She took my plate and emptied it on John's, my younger brother's, knowing the right way to get me mad. That's the trouble with me: I'm not clever. I could have bashed our John's face in and snatched it back, except the little bastard had gobbled it up, and Dad was sitting by the fire, behind his paper with one tab lifted. "You can't get me out to wok quick enough, can you?" was all I could say at Mam.

Dad chipped in, put down his paper. "Listen: no wok, no grub. So get out and look for a job tomorrow, and don't come back till you've got one."

Going to the bike factory to ask for a job meant getting up early, just as if I was back at school; there didn't seem any point in getting older. My old man was a good worker though, and I knew in my bones and brain that I took after him. At the school garden the teacher used to say: "Colin, you're the best worker I've got, and you'll get on when you leave"—after I'd spent a couple of hours digging spuds while all the others had been larking about trying to run each other over with the lawn-rollers. Then the teacher would sell the spuds off at threepence a pound and what did I get out of it? Bogger-all. Yet I liked the work because it wore me out; and I always feel pretty good when I'm worn out.

I knew you had to go to work though, and that rough work was best. I saw a picture once about a revolution in Russia, about the workers taking over everything (like Dad wants to) and they lined everybody up and made them hold their hands out and the working blokes went up and down looking at them. Anybody whose hands was lily-white was taken away and shot. The others was O.K. Well, if ever that happened in this country, I'd be O.K., and that made me feel better when a few days later I was walking down the street in overalls at half-past seven in the morning with the rest of them. One side of my face felt lively and interested in what I was in for, but the other side was crooked and sorry for itself, so that a neighbour got a front view of my whole clock and called with a wide laugh, a gap I'd like to have seen a few inches lower down—in her neck: "Never mind, Colin, it ain't all that bad."

The man on the gate took me to the turnery. The noise hit me like a boxing-glove as I went in, but I kept on walking straight into it without flinching, feeling it reach right into my guts as if to wrench them out and use them as garters. I was handed over to the foreman; then the foreman passed me on to the toolsetter; and the toolsetter took me to another youth—so that I began to feel like a hot wallet.

The youth led me to a cupboard, opened it, and gave me a sweeping brush. "Yo' do that gangway," he said, "and I'll do this one." My gangway was wider, but I didn't bother to mention it. "Bernard," he said, holding out his hand, "that's me. I go on a machine next week, a drill."

"How long you been on this sweeping?" I wanted to know, bored with it already.

"Three months. Every lad gets put on sweeping first, just to get 'em used to the place." Bernard was small and thin, older than me. We took to each other. He had round bright eyes and dark wavy hair, and spoke in a quick way as if he'd stayed at school longer than he had. He was idle, and I thought him sharp and clever, maybe because his mam dad died when he was three. He'd been brought up by an asthmatic auntie who'd not only spoiled him but let him run wild as well, he told me later when we sat supping from our tea mugs. He'd quietened down now though, and butter wouldn't melt in his mouth, he said with a wink. I couldn't think why this was, after all his stories about him being a mad-head—which put me off him at first, though after a bit he was my mate, and that was that.

We was talking one day, and Bernard said the thing he wanted to buy most in the world was a gram and lots of jazz records—New Orleans style. He was saving up and had already got ten quid.

"Me," I said, "I want a bike, to get out at week-ends up Trent. A shop on Arkwright Street sells good 'uns second hand."

I went back to my sweeping. It was a fact I've always wanted a bike. Speed gave me a thrill. Malcolm Campbell was my bigshot—but I'd settle for a two-wheeled pushbike. I'd once borrowed my cousin's and gone down Balloon House Hill so quick I passed a bus. I'd often thought how easy it would be to pinch a bike: look in a shop window until a bloke leaves his bike to go into the same shop, then nip in just before him and ask for something you knew they hadn't got; then walk out whistling to the bike at the kerb and ride off as if it's yours while the bloke's still in the shop. I'd brood for hours: fly home on it, enamel it, file off the numbers, turn the handlebars round, change the pedals, take lamps off or put them on . . . only, no, I thought, I'll be honest and save up for one when I get forced out to work, worse luck.

But work turned out to be a better life than school. I kept as hard at it as I could, and got on well with the blokes because I used to spout about how rotten the wages was and how hard the bosses slaved us—which made me popular you can bet. Like my old man always says, I told them: "At home, when you've got a headache, mash* a pot of tea.

*Nottinghamshire dialect = brew.

At work, when you've got a headache, strike." Which brought a few laughs.

Bernard was put on his drill, and one Friday while he was cleaning it down I stood waiting to cart his rammel off. "Are you still saving up for that bike, then?" he asked, pushing steel dust away with a handbrush.

"Course I am. But I'm a way off getting one yet. They rush you a fiver at that shop. Guaranteed, though."

He worked on for a minute or two then, as if he'd got a birthday present or was trying to spring a good surprise on me, said without turning round: "I've made up my mind to sell my bike."

"I didn't know you'd got one."

"Well"—a look on his face as if there was a few things I didn't know—"I bus it to work: it's easier." Then in a pallier voice: "I got it last Christmas, from my auntie. But I want a record player now."

My heart was thumping. I knew I hadn't got enough, but: "How much do you want for it?"

He smiled. "It ain't how much I want for the bike, it's how much more dough I need to get the gram and a couple of discs."

I saw Trent Valley spread out below me from the top of Carlton Hill—fields and villages, and the river like a white scarf dropped from a giant's neck. "How much do you need, then?"

He took his time about it, as if still having to reckon it up. "Fifty bob." I'd only got two quid—so the giant snatched his scarf away and vanished. Then Bernard seemed in a hurry to finish the deal: "Look, I don't want to mess about, I'll let it go for two pounds five. You can borrow the other five bob."

"I'll do it then," I said, and Bernard shook my hand like he was going away in the army. "It's a deal. Bring the dough in the morning, and I'll bike it to wok."

Dad was already in when I got home, filling the kettle at the scullery tap. I don't think he felt safe without there was a kettle on the gas. "What would you do if the world suddenly ended, Dad?" I once asked when he was in a good mood. "Mash some tea and watch it," he said. He poured me a cup.

"Lend's five bob, Dad, till Friday."

He slipped the cosy on. "What do you want to borrow money for?" I told him. "Who from?" he asked.

"My mate at wok."

He passed me the money. "Is it a good 'un?"

"I ain't seen it yet. He's bringing it in the morning."

"Make sure the brakes is safe."

Bernard came in half an hour late, so I wasn't able to see the bike till dinner-time. I kept thinking he'd took bad and wouldn't come at all, but suddenly he was stooping at the door to take his clips off—so's I'd know he'd got his—my—bike. He looked paler than usual, as if he'd been up the canal-bank, all night with a piece of skirt and caught a bilious-bout. I paid him at dinner-time. "Do you want a receipt for it?" he laughed. It was no time to lark about. I gave it a short test around the factory, then rode it home.

The next three evenings, for it was well in to summer, I rode a dozen miles out into the country, where fresh air smelt like cowshit and the land was coloured different, was wide open and windier than in streets. Marvellous. It was like a new life starting up, as if till then I'd been tied by a mile long rope round the ankle to home. Whistling along lanes I planned trips to Skegness, wondering how many miles I could make in a whole day. If I pedalled like mad, bursting my lungs for fifteen hours I'd reach London where I'd never been. It was like sawing through the bars in clink. It was a good bike as well, a few years old, but a smart racer with lamps and saddlebag and a pump that went. I thought Bernard was a bit loony parting with it at that price, but I supposed that that's how blokes are when they get dead set on a gram and discs. They'd sell their own mother, I thought, enjoying a mad dash down from Canning Circus, weaving between the cars for kicks.

"What's it like, having a bike?" Bernard asked, stopping to slap me on the back—as jolly as I'd ever seen him, yet in a kind of way that don't happen between pals.

"You should know," I said. "Why? It's all right, ain't it? The wheels are good, aren't they?"

An insulted look came into his eyes. "You can give it back if you like. I'll give you your money."

"I don't want it," I said. I could no more part with it than my right arm, and he knew it. "Got the gram yet?" And he told me about it for the next half-hour. It had got so many dials for this and that he made it sound like a space ship. We was both satisfied, which was the main thing.

That same Saturday I went to the barber's for my monthly D.A. and when I came out I saw a bloke getting on my bike to ride it away. I tagged him on the shoulder, my fist flashing red for danger.

"Off," I said sharp, ready to smash the thieving bastard. He turned to me. A funny sort of thief, I couldn't help thinking, a respectable-looking bloke of about forty wearing glasses and shiny shoes, smaller than me, with a moustache. Still, the swivel-eyed sinner was taking my bike.

"I'm boggered if I will," he said, in a quiet way so that I thought he was a bit touched. "It's my bike, anyway."

"It bloody-well ain't," I swore, "and if you don't get off I'll crack you one."

A few people gawked at us. The bloke didn't mess about and I can understand it now. "Missis," he called, "just go down the road to that copperbox and ask a policeman to come up 'ere, will you? This is my bike, and this young bogger nicked it."

I was strong for my age. "You sodding fibber," I cried, pulling him clean off the bike so's it clattered to the pavement. I picked it up to ride away, but the bloke got me round the waist, and it was more than I could do to take him off up the road as well, even if I wanted to. Which I didn't.

"Fancy robbing a working-man of his bike," somebody called out from the crowd of idle bastards now collected. I could have mowed them down.

But I didn't get a chance. A copper came, and the man was soon flicking out his wallet, showing a bill with the number of the bike on it: proof right enough. But I still thought he'd made a mistake. "You can tell us all about that at the Guildhall," the copper said to me.

I don't know why—I suppose I want my brains testing—but I stuck to a story that I found the bike dumped at the end of the yard that morning and was on my way to give it in at a copshop, and had called for a haircut first. I think the magistrate half believed me, because the bloke knew to the minute when it was pinched, and at that time I had a perfect alibi—I was in work, proved by my clocking-in card. I knew some rat who hadn't been in work though when he should have been.

All the same, being found with a pinched bike, I got put on probation, and am still doing it. I hate old Bernard's guts for playing a trick like that on me, his mate. But it was lucky for him I hated the coppers more and wouldn't nark on anybody, not even a dog. Dad would have killed me if ever I had, though he didn't need to tell me. I could only thank God a story came to me as quick as it did, though in one way I still sometimes reckon I was barmy not to have told them how I got that bike.

There's one thing I do know. I'm waiting for Bernard to come out of borstal. He got picked up, the day after I was copped with the bike, for robbing his auntie's gas meter to buy more discs. She'd had about all she could stand from him, and thought a spell inside would do him good, if not cure him altogether. I've got a big bone to pick with him, because he owes me forty-five bob I don't care where he gets it—even if he goes out and robs another meter—but I'll get it out of him, I swear blind I will. I'll pulverise him.

Another thing about him though that makes me laugh is that, if ever there's a revolution and everybody's lined-up with their hands out, Bernard's will still be lily-white, because he's a bone-idle thieving bastard—and then we'll see how he goes on; because mine won't be lily-white, I can tell you that now. And you never know, I might even be one of the blokes picking 'em out.

The Ragman's Daughter

I was walking home with an empty suitcase one night, an up-to-date pigskin zip job I was fetching back from a pal who thought he'd borrowed it for good, and two plain-clothed coppers stopped me. They questioned me for twenty minutes, then gave up and let me go. While they had been talking to me, a smash-and-grab had taken place around the corner, and ten thousand nicker had vanished into the wide open spaces of somebody who needed it.

That's life. I was lucky my suitcase had nothing but air in it. Sometimes I walk out with a box of butter and cheese from the warehouse I work at, but for once that no-good God was on my side—trying to make up for the times he's stabbed me in the back maybe. But if the coppers had had a word with me a few nights later they'd have found me loaded with high-class provision snap.

My job is unloading cheeses as big as beer barrels off lorries that come in twice a week from the country. They draw in at the side door of the warehouse, and me and a couple of mates roll our sleeves up and shoulder them slowly down the gangplank into the special part set aside for cheeses. We once saw, after checking the lists, that there was one cheese extra, so decided to share it out between a dozen of us and take it home to our wives and families. The question came up as to which cheese we should get rid of, and the chargehand said: "Now, all look around for the cheese that the rats have started to go for, and that's the one we'll carve between us, because you can bet your bottom dollar that that's the best."

It was a load of choice Dalbeattie, and I'd never tasted any cheese so delicious. For a long time my wife would say: "When are you going to get us some more of that marvellous cheese, Tony?" And whatever I did take after that never seemed to satisfy them, though every time I went out with a chunk of cheese or a fist of butter I was risking my job, such as it is. Once for a treat I actually bought a piece of Dalbeattie from another shop, but they knew it wasn't stolen so it didn't taste as good as the other that the rats had pointed out to us. It happens now and again at the warehouse that a bloke takes some butter and the police nab him. They bring him back and he gets the push. Fancy getting the push for half a pound of butter. I'd be ashamed to look my mates in the eye again, and would be glad I'd got the sack so's I wouldn't have to.

The first thing I stole was at infants school when I was five. They gave us cardboard coins to play with, pennies, shillings, half-crowns, stiff and almost hard to bend, that we were supposed to exchange for bricks and pieces of chalk. This lesson was called Buying and Selling. Even at the time I remember feeling that there was something not right about the game, yet only pouting and playing it badly because I wasn't old enough to realise what it was. But when I played well I ended up the loser, until I learned quickly that one can go beyond skill: at the end of the next afternoon I kept about half a dozen of the coins (silver I noticed later) in my pocket when the teacher came round to collect them back.

"Some is missing," she said, in that plummy voice that sent shivers down my spine and made me want to give them up. But I resisted my natural inclinations and held out. "Someone hasn't given their money back," she said. "Come along, children, own up, or I'll keep you in after all the other classes have gone home."

I was hoping she'd search me, but she kept us in for ten minutes, and I went home with my pockets full. That night I was caught by a shopkeeper trying to force the coins into his fag and chewing-gum machines. He dragged me home and the old man lammed into me. So, sobbing up to bed, I learned at an early age that money meant trouble as well.

Next time at school I helped myself to bricks, but teacher saw my bulging pockets and took them back, then threw me into the playground, saying I wasn't fit to be at school. This showed me that it was always safest to go for money.

Once, an uncle asked what I wanted to be when I grew up, and I answered: "A thief". He bumped me, so I decided, whenever anybody else asked that trick question to say: "An honest man" or "An engine driver". I stole money from my mother's purse, or odd coppers left lying around the house for gas or electricity, and so I got batted for that as well as for saying I wanted to be a thief when I grew up. I began to see that really I was getting clobbered for the same thing, which made me keep my trap shut on the one hand, and not get caught on the other.

In spite of the fact that I nicked whatever I could lay my hands on without too much chance of getting caught, I didn't like possessing things. Suits, a car, watches—as soon as I nicked something and got clear away, I lost interest in it. I broke into an office and came out with two typewriters, and after having them at home for a day I borrowed a car and dropped them over Trent bridge one dark night. If the cops cared to dredge the river about there they'd get a few surprises. What I like most is the splash stuff makes when I drop it in: that plunge into water of something heavy—such as a TV set, a cash register and once, best of all, a motorbike—which makes a dull exploding noise and has the same effect on me as booze (which I hate) because it makes my head spin. Even a week later, riding on a bus, I'll suddenly twitch and burst out laughing at the thought of it, and some posh trot will tut-tut, saying: "These young men! Drunk at eleven in the morning! What they want is to be in the army."

If I lost all I have in the world I wouldn't worry much. If I was to go across the road for a packet of fags one morning and come back to see the house clapping its hands in flames with everything I owned burning inside I'd turn my back without any thought or regret and walk away, even if my jacket and last ten-bob note were in the flames as well.

What I'd like, believe it or not, is to live in a country where I didn't like thieving and where I didn't want to thieve, a place where everybody felt the same way because they all had only the same as everyone else—even if it wasn't much. Jail is a place like this, though it's not the one I'd find agreeable because you aren't free there. The place that fills my mind would be the same as in jail because everybody would have the same, but being free as well they wouldn't want to nick what bit each had got. I don't know what sort of system that would be called.

While as a youth I went out with girls, I used to like thieving more. The best of all was when I got a young girl to come thieving with me. The right sort was better than any mate I could team up with, more exciting and safe.

I met Doris outside a fish-and-chip shop on Ilkeston Road. Going in to get a supply for supper she dropped her purse, and a few obstinate shekels rolled into the road. "Don't worry," I said, "I'll find them, duck."

A couple of other youths wanted to help, but I got one by the elbow. "Bale out. She's my girl-friend. You'll get crippled for life."

"All right, Tony," he laughed. "I didn't know it was you."

I picked her money up: "This is the lot"—followed her into the light of the fish-and-chip shop where I could see what she was made of. "I'm going for some chips as well," I said, so as not to put her off.

"Thanks for getting my money. I have butterfingers sometimes." Her hair was the colour of butter, yellow and reaching for her shoulders, where my hands wanted to be. We stood in the queue. I'd just eaten a bundle of fish-and-chips downtown, so even the smell in this joint turned my guts. "Haven't I seen you somewhere before?" I asked.

"You might, for all I know. I've been around nearly as long as you have."

"Where do you live, then?"

"Up Churchfield lane."

"I'll see you home."

"You won't." She was so fair and goodlooking that I almost lost heart, though not enough to stop me answering: "You might drop your purse again." I didn't know whether I'd passed her on the street some time, dreamed about her, or seen her drifting across the television screen in a shampoo advertisement between 'Blood Gun' and 'The Kremlin Strikes Again'. Her skin was smooth, cheeks a bit meaty, eyes blue, small nose and lips also fleshy but wearing a camouflage of orange-coloured lipstick that made me want to kiss them even more than if it had been flag-red. She stood at the counter with a vacant, faraway look in her eyes, the sort that meant she had a bit more thought in her rather than the other way round. She gave a little sniff at the billowing clouds of chip steam doubled in size because of mirrors behind the sizzling bins. It was impossible to tell whether or not she liked the smell.

"You're a long way from Churchfield Lane," I said. "Ain't you got chip shops up that part?"

"Dad says they do good fish here," she told me. "So I come to get him some, as a favour."

"It's better at Rawson's though, downtown. You ought to let me take you there some time—for a supper. You'd enjoy it."

It was her turn at the counter. "I'm busy these days. Two shillings worth of chips and six fish, please."

"Where do you work, then?"

"I don't."

I laughed: "Neither do I."

She took her bundle: "Thank you very much"—turned to me: "You won't be able to take me out then, will you?"

I edged a way back to the door, and we stood on the pavement. "You're a torment, as well as being good-looking. I've still got money, even if I don't go to work right now." We walked across the road, and all the time I was waiting for her to tell me to skid, hoping she would yet not wanting her to. "Does it fall from heaven, then?"

"No, I nick it."

She half believed me. "I'll bet you do. Where from?"

"It all depends. Anywhere." I could already see myself taking her the whole way home—if I kept my trap flapping.

"I've never stolen anything in my life," she said, "but I've often wanted to."

"If you stick around I'll show you a few things."

She laughed: "I might be scared."

"Not with me. We'll go out one night and see what we can do."

"Fast worker. We could do it for kicks, though."

"It's better to do it for money," I said, dead strict on this.

"What's the difference? It's stealing."

I'd never thought about it this way before. "Maybe it is. But it's still not the same."

"If you do it for kicks," she went on, "you don't get caught so easily."

"There's no point in doing something just for kicks," I argued. "It's a waste of time."

"Well," she said, "I'll tell you what. You do it for money, and I'll do it for kicks. Then we'll both be satisfied."

"Fine," I said, taking her arm, "that sounds reasonable."

She lived in a big old house just off Churchfield Lane, and I even got a kiss out of her before she went into the garden and called me a soft good night. Doris, she had said, my name is Doris.

I thought she was joking about stealing stuff for kicks, but I met her a few days later outside a cinema, and when the show was over and we stood by a pavement where five roads met, she said: "I suppose you just prowl around until you see something that's easy and quiet."

"More or less"—not showing my surprise. "It might be a bit harder than that though." I held up a jack knife, that looked like a hedgehog with every blade splayed out: "That one ain't for opening pop bottles; and this one ain't for getting stones out of horses hoofs either. A useful little machine, this is."

"I thought you used hairgrips?" She was treating it like a joke, but I said deadpan: "Sometimes. Depends on the lock." A copper walked across the road towards us, and with every flat footstep I closed a blade of the knife, slipping it into my pocket before he was half-way over. "Come on," I said, lighting a fag, and heading towards Berridge Road.

The overhead lights made us look TB, as if some big government scab had made a mistake on the telephone and had too much milk tipped into the sea. We even stopped talking at the sight of each other's fag-ash faces, but after a while the darker side streets brought us back to life, and every ten yards I got what she'd not been ready to give on the back seat of the pictures: a fully-fledged passionate kiss. Into each went all my wondering at why a girl like this should want to come out on nightwork with a lout called me.

"You live in a big house," I said when we walked on. "What does your old man do?"

"He's a scrapdealer."

"Scrapdealer?" It seemed funny, somehow. "No kidding?"

"You know—rag and metal merchant. Randall's on Orston Road."

I laughed, because during my life as a kid that was the place I'd taken scrap-iron and jamjars, lead and woollens to, and her old man was the bloke who'd traded with me—a deadbeat skinflint with a pound note sign between his eyes and breathing LSD all over the place. Dead at the brain and crotch the fat gett drove a maroon Jaguar in an old lounge suit. I'd seen him one day scatter a load of kids in the street, pumping that screaming button-hooter before he got too close, and as they bulletted out of his way throw a fistful of change after them. He nearly smashed into a lamp-post because such sudden and treacherous generosity put him off his steering.

"What's funny about it?" she wanted to know.

"I'm surprised, that's all."

"I told a girl at school once that my dad was a scrap-dealer, and she laughed, just like you did. I don't see what's funny about it at all." You stupid bastard, I called myself, laughing for nothing when before you'd been getting marvellous kisses from her. A black cat shot through the light of a lamp-post, taking good luck with it.

"He's better off than most people, so maybe you laugh because you're jealous."

"Not me," I said, trying to make amends. "Another reason I laughed, if you want to know the truth, is that I've always wanted to be a scrapdealer, but so far I've never known how to get started. It was just the coincidence." While she was wondering whether to believe me I tried changing the subject: "What sort of a school did you go to where they'd laugh at a thing like that?"

"I still go," she said, "a grammar school. I leave at the end of the year, though." A school kid, I thought. Still, she's a posh one, so she can be nearly seventeen, though she looks at least as old as me, which is eighteen and a half. "I'll be glad to leave school, anyway. I want to be independent. I'm always in top class though, so in a sense I like it as well. Funny."

"You want to get a job, you mean?"

"Sure. Of course. I'll go to a secretarial college. Dad says he'd let me."

"Sounds all right. You'll be set for life, the way you're going." We were walking miles, pacing innumerable streets out of our systems, a slow arm-in-arm zig-zag through the darkening neighbourhood. It was a night full of star holes after a day of rain, a windy sky stretching into a huge flow over the rising ground of Forest Fields and Hyson Green and Basford, through Mapperly to Redhill and carried away by some red doubledecker loaded with colliers vanishing into the black night of Sherwood. We made a solitary boat in this flood of small houses, packed together like the frozen teeth of sharp black waves and, going from one lighthouse lamp-post to another, the district seemed an even bigger stretch than the area I was born and brought up in.

An old woman stood on a doorstep saying: "Have you got a fag, my duck? I'd be ever so grateful if you could manage it." She looked about ninety, and when I handed her one she lit up as if ready to have a nervous breakdown. "Thanks, my love. I hope you'll be happy, the pair of you."

"Same to you, missis," I said as we went off.

"Aren't old women funny?" Doris said.

We kissed at every corner, and whenever it seemed I might not she reminded me by a tug at my linked arm. She wore slacks and a head scarf, a three-quarter leather coat and flat-heeled lace-ups, as if this was her idea of a break-and-entry rig. She looked good in it, stayed serious and quiet for most of the walking, so that all we did now and again was move into a clinch for a good bout of tormenting kisses. She moaned softly sometimes, and I wanted to go further than lipwork, but how could we in a solid wide open street where someone walking through would disturb us? With the air so sweet and long lasting, I knew it would be a stretch past her bed time before she finally landed home that night. Yet I didn't care, felt awake and marvellous, full of love for all the world—meaning her first and then myself, and it showed in our kisses as we went at a slow rate through the streets, arms fast around each other like Siamese twins.

Across the main road stretched a wall covering the yard of a small car-body workshop. As soon as I saw it my left leg began trembling and the kneecap of my right to twitch, so I knew this was the first place we'd go into together. I always got scared as soon as the decision was made, though it never took long for fright to get chased off as I tried to fathom a way into the joint.

I told Doris: "You go to the end of the street and keep conk. I'll try to force this gate, and whistle if I do. If you see anybody coming walk back here, and we'll cuddle up as if we're courting." She did as she was told, while I got to work on the gate lock, using first the bottle-opener and then the nail-file, then the spike. With a bit more play it snapped back, and I whistled. We were in the yard.

There was no word said from beginning to end. If I'd been doing it with a mate you'd have heard scufflings and mutterings, door-rattlings and shoulder-knocks and the next thing we'd be in a cop car on our way to Guildhall. But now, our limbs and eyes acted together, as if controlled by one person that was neither of us, a sensation I'd never known before. A side door opened and we went between a line of machines into a partitioned office to begin a quiet and orderly search. I'd been once in a similar place with a pal, and the noise as we pulled drawers and slung typewriters about, and took pot shots with elastic and paperclips at light bulbs was so insane that it made me stop and silence him as well after five minutes. But now there wasn't a scratch or click anywhere.

Still with no word I walked to the door, and Doris came after me. In two seconds we were back on the street, leaning against the workshop wall to fill each of our mouths with such kisses that I knew I loved her, and that from then on I was in the fire, floating, burning, feeling the two of us ready to explode if we didn't get out of this to where we could lie down. Nothing would stop us, because we already matched and fused together, not even if we fell into a river or snowbank.

There was no gunning of feet from the factory so that a lawful passing pedestrian could suspect we were up to no good and squeal for the coppers. After five minutes snogging we walked off, as if we'd just noticed how late it was and remembered we had to be at work in the morning. At the main road I said: "What did you get?"

She took a bundle of pound notes from her pocket: "This. What about you?"

I emptied a large envelope of postage stamps and cheques: "Useless. You got the kitty, then."

"I guess so," she said, not sounding too full of joy.

"Not bad for a beginner. A school kid, as well!" I gave her half the stamps and she handed me half the money—which came to twenty quid apiece. We homed our way the couple of miles back, sticking one or two stamps (upside down) on each of the corners turned. "I don't write letters," I laughed. It was a loony action, but I have to do something insane on every job, otherwise there's no chance of getting caught, and if there's no chance of getting caught, there's no chance of getting away. I explained this to Doris, who said she'd never heard such a screwy idea, but that she was nearly convinced about it because I was more experienced than she was. Luckily the stamps ran out, otherwise the trail would have gone right through our back door, up the stairs and into my bedroom, the last one on my pillow hidden by my stupid big head. I felt feather-brained and obstinate, knowing that even if the world rolled over me I wouldn't squash.

By the banks of the Leen at Bobber's Mill we got under the fence and went down where nobody could see us. It was after midnight, and quiet but for the sound of softly rolling cold water a few feet off, as black as heaven for the loving we had to do.

Doris called for me at home, turned the corner, and came down our cobbled street on a horse. My brother Paul ran in and said: "Come and look at this woman (he was only nine) on a horse, our Tony"—and having nothing better to do while waiting for Doris but flip through the *Mirror* I strode to the yard-end. It was a warm day, dust in the wind making a lazy atmosphere around the eyes, smoke sneaking off at right-angles to chimneys and telly masts. By the pavement I looked down the street and saw nothing but a man going across to the shop in shirtsleeves and braces, then swivelling my eyes the other way I saw this girl coming down the street on a walking horse.

It was a rare sight, because she was beautiful, had blonde hair like Lady Godiva except that she was dressed in riding slacks and a white shirt that set a couple of my Ted mates whistling at her, though most stayed quiet with surprise—and envy—when the horse pulled up at our yard-end and Doris on it said hello to me. It was hard to believe that last night we'd broken into a factory, seemed even more far gone than in a dream; though what we'd done later by the river was real enough, especially when I caught that smell of scent and freshness as she bent down from the horse's neck. "Why don't you come in for a cup of tea? Bring your horse in for a crust as well."

It was a good filly, the colour of best bitter, with eyes like priceless damsons that were alive because of their reflector-light in them. The only horses seen on our street—pulling coal carts or bread vans—had gone to the knackers' yards years ago. I took the bridle and led it up the yard, Doris talking softly from high up and calling it Marian, guiding it over the smooth stones. A man came out of a lavatory and had a fit in his eyes when he nearly bumped into it. "It wain't bite you, George," I laughed.

"I'll have it for Sunday dinner if it does," he said, stalking off.

"It wain't be the first time," I called. My mother was washing clothes at the scullery sink, and it pushed its head to the window for a good look—until she glanced up "Tony! What have you got there!"

"Only a horse, mam," I shouted back. "It's all right: I ain't nicked it"—as she came out drying her hands.

"A friend of mine come to see me," I told her, introducing Doris, who dropped to her proper size on the asphalt. My mother patted the horse as if it were a stray dog, then went in for a piece of bread. She'd been brought up in the country, and liked animals.

"We had a good time last night," I said to Doris, thinking about it.

"Not bad. What shall we do with the money?"

"Spend it."

Our fence was rickety, looked as if it would fall down when she tethered the horse to it. "Funny," she said. "But what on?"

"How much does a horse cost?" I asked, tapping its nose.

"I'm not sure. Dad got me Marian. More than twenty pounds, though." I was disappointed, had pictured us riding in the country, overland to Langley Mill and Matlock Bath without using a road once, the pair of us making a fine silhouette on some lonely skyline. Then as on the films we'd wind our way far down into the valley and get lodgings at a pub or farmhouse. Bit by bit we'd edge to Scotland and maybe at the end of all our long wandering by horse we'd get a job as man and wife working a light house. Set on a rock far out at sea, the waves would bash at it like mountains of snow, and we'd keep the lights going, still loving each other and happy even though we hadn't had a letter or lettuce in six months.

The sun shone over our backyards, and I was happy anyway: "I'll just get rid of my dough, enjoy myself. I'm out of work, so it'll keep me for a month."

"I hope we don't have to wait that long before doing it again," she said, brushing her hair back.

"We'll go tonight, if you like. I'll bet the coppers don't know we went into that factory yet." My mother came out with a bag of crusts for the horse: "I've just made a pot of tea," she said. "Go and pour it, Tony."

When we got behind the door I pulled Doris to me and kissed her. She kissed me, as well. Not having to chase and fight for it made it seem like real love.

We went on many 'expeditions', as Doris called them. I even got a makeshift job at a factory in case anybody should wonder how I was living. Doris asked if it would be O.K. to bring a school pal with us one night, and this caused our first argument. I said she was loony to think of such a thing, and did she imagine I was running a school for cowing crime, or summat? I hoped she hadn't mentioned our prowling nights to anybody else—though she hadn't, as it turned out, and all she'd wanted was to see if this particular girl at her school would be able to do this sort of job as cool as she could. "Well, drop it," I said, sharp. "We do all right by oursens, so let's keep it to oursens."

Having been brought up as the ragman's daughter and never wanting for dough, she had hardly played with the kids in the street. She hadn't much to do with those at school either, for they lived mostly in new houses and bungalows up Wollaton and would never come to Radford to call on her. So she'd been lonely in a way I never had been.

Her parents lived in a house off Churchfield Lane, a big ancient one backing its yards (where the old man still kept some of his scrap mountains) on to the Leen. Her dad had worked like a navvy all day and every day of his life, watching each farthing even after he was rich enough to retire like a lord. I don't know what else he could have done. Sucked ice-cream at the seaside? Gardened his feet off? Fished himself to death? He preferred to stick by sun, moon or electric light sorting metal or picking a bone with his own strength because, being a big and satisfied man, that was all he felt like doing—and who could blame him? Doris told me he was mean with most things, though not with her. She could have what she liked.

"Get a hundred, then," I said.

But she just smiled and thought that wouldn't be right, that she'd only have from him what he gave her because she liked it better that way.

Every week-end she came to our house, on her horse except when the weather was bad. If nobody else was in she fastened her steed to the fence and we went up to my bedroom, got undressed and had the time of our lives. She had a marvellous figure, small breasts for her age, yet wide hips as if they'd finished growing before anything else of her. I always had the idea she felt better out of her clothes, realising maybe that no clothes, even if expensive like gold, could ever match her birthday suit for a perfect fit that was always the height of fashion. We'd put a few Acker Bilk's low on my record player and listen for a while with nothing on, getting drowsy and warmed up under the usual talk and kisses. Then after having it we'd sit and talk more, maybe have it again before mam or dad shuffled and whinnied, it was like being in a cottage bedroom, alone with her and in the country. If it was sunny and warm as well and a sudden breeze pushed air into the room and flipped a photo of some pop singer off the shelf and fell softly at our bare skins I'd feel like a stallion, as fit and strong as a buck African and we'd have it over and over so that my legs wobbled as I walked back down the stairs.

People got used to seeing her ride down the street, and they'd say: "Hello, duck"—adding: "He's in"—meaning me—"I just saw him come back from the shop with a loaf." George Clark asked when I was going to get married, and when I shouted that I didn't know he laughed: "I expect you've got to find a place big enough for the horse as well, first." At which I told him to mind his own effing business.

Yet people were glad that Doris rode down our street on a horse, and I sensed that because of it they even looked up to me more—or maybe they only noticed me in a different way to being carted off by the coppers. Doris was pleased when a man coming out of the bookie's called after her: "Hey up, Lady Luck!"—waving a five-pound note in the air.

Often we'd go down town together, ending up at the pictures, or in a pub over a bitter or babycham. But nobody dreamed what we got up to before finally parting for our different houses. If we pinched fags or food or clothes we'd push what was possible through the letter-box of the first house we came to, or if it was too big we'd leave good things in litter-bins for some poor tramp or tatter to find. We were hardly ever seen, and never caught, on these expeditions, as if love made us invisible, ghosts without sound walking hand in hand between dark streets until we came to some factory, office, lock-up shop or house that we knew was empty of people—and every time this happened I remember the few seconds of surprise, not quite fear, at both of us knowing exactly what to do. I would stand a moment at this surprise—thankful, though waiting for it to go—until she squeezed my hand, and I was moving again, to finish getting in.

I was able to buy a motorbike, a secondhand powerful speedster, and when Doris called she'd leave her horse in our backyard, and we'd nip off for a machine-spin towards Stanton Ironworks, sliding into a full ton once we topped Balloon House Hill and had a few miles of straight and flat laid out for us like an airport runway. Slag heaps looked pale blue in summer, full triangles set like pyramid-targets way ahead and I'd swing towards them between leaf hedges of the country road, hoping they'd keep that far-off vacant colour, as if they weren't real. They never did though, and I lost them at a dip and bend, and when next in sight they were grey and useless and scabby, too real to look good any more.

On my own I rode with L plates, and took a test so as to get rid of them on the law's side of the law, but I didn't pass because I never was good at examinations. Roaring along with Doris straight as goldenrod behind, and hearing noises in the wind tunnel I made whisper sweet nothings into our four ear-holes, was an experience we loved, and I'd shout: "You can't ride this fast on a horse"—and listen to the laugh she gave, which meant she liked to do both.

She once said: "Why don't we go on an expedition on your bike?" and I answered: "Why don't we do one on your hoss?" adding: "Because it'd spoil everything, wouldn't it?"

She laughed: "You're cleverer than I think."

"No kidding," I said, sarky. "If only you could see yoursen as I can see you, and if only I could see mysen as you can see me, things would be plainer for us, wouldn't they?"

I couldn't help talking. We'd stopped the bike and were leaning on a bridge wall, with nothing but trees and a narrow lane roundabout, and the green-glass water of a canal below. Her arm was over my shoulder, and my arm was around her waist: "I wonder if they would?" she said.

"I don't know. Let's go down into them trees."

"What for?"

"Because I love you."

She laughed again: "Is that all?"—then took my arm: "Come on, then."

We played a game for a long time in our street, where a gang of us boys held fag lighters in a fair wind, flicking them on and off and seeing which light stayed on longest. It was a stupid game because everything was left to chance, and though this can be thrilling you can't help but lose by it in the end. This game was all the rage for weeks, before we got fed up, or our lighters did, I forget which. Sooner or later every lighter goes out or gives in; or a wind in jackboots jumps from around the corner and kicks it flat—and you get caught under the avalanche of the falling world.

One summer's week-end we waited in a juke-box coffee bar for enough darkness to settle over the streets before setting out. Doris wore jeans and sweatshirt, and I was without a jacket because of the warm night. Also due to the warmth we didn't walk the miles we normally did before nipping into something, which was a pity because a lot of hoof-work put our brains and bodies into tune for such quiet jobs, relaxed and warmed us so that we became like cats, alert and ready at any warning sound to duck or scram. Now and again the noise of the weather hid us—thunder, snow, drizzle, wind, or even the fact that clouds were above made enough noise for us to operate more safely than on this night of open sky with a million ears and eyes of copper stars cocked and staring. Every footstep deafened me, and occasionally on our casual stroll we'd stop to look at each other, stand a few seconds under the wall of a side-lit empty street, then walk on hand in hand. I wanted to whistle (softly) or sing a low tune to myself, for, though I felt uneasy at the open dumb night, it was also the kind of night that left me confident and full of energy, and when these things joined I was apt to get a bit reckless. But I held back, slowed my heart and took in every detail of each same street—so as to miss no opportunity, as they drummed into us at school. "I feel as if I've had a few," I said, in spite of my resolution.

"So do I."

"Or as if we'd just been up in my room and had it together."

"I don't feel like going far, though," she said.

"Tired, duck?"

"No, but let's go home. I don't feel like it tonight."

I wondered what was wrong with her, saying: "I'll walk you back and we'll call it a day."

In the next street I saw a gate leading to the rear yard of a shop, and I was too spun up to go home without doing anything at all: "Let's just nip in here. You needn't come, duck. I wain't-be five minutes."

"O.K." She smiled, though my face was already set at that loot-barrier. It wasn't very high, and when I was on top she called: "Give me a hand up."

"Are you sure?"

"Of course I am." It was the middle of a short street, and lamp-posts at either end didn't shed radiance this far up. I got to the back door and, in our usual quiet way, the lock was forced and we stood in a smell of leather, polish and cardboard boxes.

"It's a shoe shop," Doris said. I felt my path across the storehouse behind the selling part of the shop, by racks and racks of shoe boxes, touching paper and balls of string on a corner table.

We went round it like blind people in the dark a couple of times just to be sure we didn't miss a silent cashbox cringing and holding its breath as our fingers went by. People on such jobs often miss thousands through hurrying or thinking the coppers are snorting down their necks. My old man insists I get the sack from one firm after another because I'm not thorough enough in my work, but if he could have seen me on this sort of task he'd have to think again.

There was nothing in the backroom. I went into the shop part and in ten seconds flat was at the till, running my fingers over them little plastic buttons as if I was going to write a letter to my old man explaining just how thorough I could be at times. To make up for the coming small clatter of noise I held my breath—hoping both would average out to make it not heard. A couple of no-good night owls walked by outside, then I turned the handle and felt the till drawer thump itself towards my guts. It's the best punch in the world, like a tabby cat boxing you with its paw, soft and loaded as it slides out on ballbearing rollers.

My hand made the lucky dip, lifted a wad of notes from under a spring-weight, and the other scooped up silver, slid it into my pocket as if it were that cardboard money they used to lend us at infants' school to teach us how to be good shoppers and happy savers—not rattling good coin ready for grown-ups to get rid of. I went to the back room and stood by the exit to make sure all was clear.

The light went on, a brilliant blue striplight flooding every corner of the room. I froze like a frog that's landed in grass instead of water. When I could speak I said to Doris: "What did you do that for?"—too scared to be raving mad.

"Because I wanted to." She must have sensed how much I felt like bashing her, because: "Nobody can see it from the street"—which could have been true, but even so.

"Kicks are kicks," I said, "but this is a death trap."

"Scared?" she smiled.

"Just cool"—feeling anything but. "I've got about fifty quid in my pocket."

She stood against a wall of shoe boxes, and even a telly ad couldn't have gone deeper into my guts than the sight of Doris now. Yellow arms of light turned full on her left me in the shade—which was fine, for I expected to see the dead mug of a copper burst in at any moment. Yet even at that I wouldn't be able to care. I felt as if music was in my head wanting to get out, as if it had come to me because I was one of those who could spin it out from me, though knowing I'd never had any say in a thing like that.

She didn't speak, stood to her full fair height and stared. I knew we were safe, that no copper would make any capture that night because the light she had switched on protected us both. We were cast-iron solid in this strong-box of shoes, and Doris knew it as well because when I couldn't help but smile she broke the spell by saying:

"I want to try some shoes on."

"What?"

"Maybe they've got some of the latest."

The idea was barmy, not so that I wanted to run like a shot stag out of the place, but so that I could have done a handstand against the wall of boxes. I lifted out an armful and set them on the floor like a game of dominoes. She chose one and opened it gently. I took up a box and split it down the middle: "Try these."

They were too small, a pair of black shiners with heels like toothpicks. "I wish the shopkeeper was here," she said, "then he could tell me where the best are. This is a waste of time."

I scoffed. "You don't want much, do you? You'd have to pay for them, then. No, we'll go through the lot and find a few pairs of Paris fashions."

"Not in this shop"—contemptuously slinging a pair of plain lace-ups to the other side of the room, enough noise to wake every rat under the skirting board. From the ladder I passed down a few choice boxes, selecting every other on the off chance of picking winners. "I should have come in skirt and stockings," she said,"then I could have told which ones suit me."

"Well, next time we go into a shoe shop I'll let you know; I'll wear an evening suit and we'll bring a transistor to do a hop with. Try these square toes. They'll go well with slacks."

They fitted but, being the wrong colour, were hurled out with the other misfits. The room was scattered with shoes, looked as if one of them Yank cyclones—Mabel or Edna or whatever you call them—had been hatched there, or as if a meeting of cripples and one-legs had been suddenly broken up by news of the four-minute warning. She still hadn't found the right pair, so went on looking as if she lived there, ordering shop-assistant me about, though I didn't mind because it seemed like a game we were playing.

"Why don't you find a pair for yourself?" she said.

"No, we'll get you fixed. I'm always well shod."

I knew that we were no longer safe in that shop and sprang to switch off the lights. "You silly fool," she cried.

Darkness put us into another world, the real one we were used to, or that I was anyway because it was hard to tell which sort of world Doris felt at home in. All she wanted, I sometimes thought, was a world with kicks, but I didn't fancy being for long at the mercy of a world in pitboots. Maybe it wore carpet slippers when dealing with her—though I shouldn't get like that now that it's been over for so long.

"Why did you switch off the light?" she yelled.

"Come on, let's get outside."

We were in the yard, Doris without any pair of shoes except those she'd come out in that evening. The skyline for me ended at the top of the gate, for a copper was coming over it, a blue-black tree trunk bending towards us about twenty yards away. Doris was frozen like a rabbit. I pushed her towards some back sheds so that she was hidden between two of them before the copper, now in the yard, spotted the commotion.

He saw me, though. I dodged to another space, then ricochetted to the safe end of the yard, and when he ran at me, stinking of fags and beer, I made a nip out of his long arms and was on the gate saddle before he could reach me.

"Stop, you little bogger," he called. "I've got you."

But all he had was one of my feet, and after a bit of tugging I left my shoe in the copper's hand. As I was racing clippitty-clop, hop-skip-and-a-jump up the street, I heard his boots rattling the boards of the gate as he got over—not, thank God, having twigged that Doris was in there and could now skip free.

I was a machine, legs fastened to my body like nuts and bolts, arms pulling me along as I ran down that empty street. I turned each corner like a flashing tadpole, heart in my head as I rattled the pavement so fast that I went from the eye of lamp-post to lamp-post in what seemed like no seconds at all. There was no worry in my head except the need to put a mile of zig-zags between that copper and me. I'd stopped hearing him only a few yards from the shoe shop gate, but it seemed that half an hour passed before I had to give up running in case I blew to pieces from the heavy bombs now getting harder all over me.

Making noises like a crazy elephant, I walked only realizing now that one of my shoes was missing. The night had fallen apart, split me and Doris from each other, and I hoped she'd made a getaway before the copper gave me up and went back to check on what I'd nicked.

I threw my other shoe over the wall of an old chapel and went home barefoot, meaning to buy myself some more next day with the fifty quid still stuck in my pocket. The shoe landed on a heap of cinders and rusting cans, and the softness of my feet on the pavement was more than made up for by the solid ringing curses my brain and heart played ping-pong with. I kept telling myself this was the end, and though I knew it was, another voice kept urging me to hope for the best and look on the bright side—like some mad deceiving parson on the telly.

I was so sure of the end that before turning into our street I dropped the fifty pound bundle through somebody's letter box and hoped that when they found it they'd not say a word to anybody about such good luck. This in fact was what happened, and by the time I was safe for a three-year lap in borstal the old woman who lived there had had an unexpected good time on the money that was, so she said, sent to her by a grateful and everloving nephew in Sheffield.

Next morning two cops came to our door, and I knew it was no good lying because they looked at me hard, as if they'd seen me on last night's television reading the news. One of them held my shoes in his hand: "Do these fit you?"

A short while before my capture Doris said, when we were kissing good night outside her front door: "I've learnt a lot since meeting you. I'm not the same person any more." Before I had time to find out what she'd learnt I was down at the cop shop and more than half-way to borstal. It was a joke, and I laughed on my way there. They never knew about Doris, so she went scot-free, riding her horse whenever she felt like it. I had that to be glad about at least. As a picture it made a stove in my guts those first black months, and as a joke I laughed over and over again, because it would never go stale on me. I'd learned a lot as well since meeting Doris, though to be honest I even now can't explain what it is. But what I learned is still in me, feeding my quieter life with energy almost without my noticing it.

I wrote to Doris from borstal but never received an answer, and even my mother couldn't tell me anything about her, or maybe wouldn't, because plenty happened to Doris that all the district knew of. Myself though, I was kept three years in the dark, suffering and going off my head at something that without this love and worry I'd have sailed through laughing. Twenty of the lads would jump on me when I raved at night, and gradually I became low and brainless and without breath like a beetle and almost stopped thinking of her, hoping that maybe she'd be waiting for me when I came out and that we'd be able to get married.

That was the hope of story books, of television and BBC; didn't belong at all to me and life and somebody like Doris. For three solid years my brain wouldn't leave me alone, came at me each night and rolled over me like a wheel of fire, so that I still sweat blood at the thought of that torture, waiting, waiting without news, like a dwarf locked in the dark. No borstal could take the credit for such punishment as this.

On coming out I pieced everything together. Doris had been pregnant when I was sent down, and three months later married a garage mechanic who had a reputation for flying around on motorbikes like a dangerous loon. Maybe that was how she prolonged the bout of kicks that had started with me, but this time it didn't turn out so well. The baby was a boy, and she named it after me. When it was two months old she went out at Christmas Eve with her husband. They were going to a dance at Derby on the motorbike and, tonning around a frosty bend, met a petrol bowser side on. Frost, darkness, and large red letters spelling PETROL were the last things she saw, and I wondered what was in her mind at that moment. Not much, because she was dead when the bowser man found her, and so was her husband. She couldn't have been much over eighteen.

"It just about killed her dad as well," my mother said, "broke his heart. I talked to him once on the street, and he said he'd allus wanted to send her to the university, she was so clever. Still, the baby went back to him."

And I went back to jail, for six months, because I opened a car door and took out a transistor radio. I don't know why I did it. The wireless was no good to me and I didn't need it. I wasn't even short of money. I just opened the car door and took out the radio and, here's what still mystifies me, I switched it on straightaway and listened to some music as I walked down the street, so that the bloke who owned the car heard it and chased after me.

But that was the last time I was in the nick—touch wood—and maybe I had to go in, because when I came out I was able to face things again, walk the streets without falling under a bus or smashing a jeweller's window for the relief of getting caught.

I got work at a sawmill, keeping the machines free of dust and wood splinters. The screaming engine noise ripping through trunks and planks was even fiercer than the battle-shindig in myself, which was a good thing during the first months I was free. I rode there each morning on a new-bought bike, to work hard before eating my dinner sand-wiches under a spreading chestnut tree. The smell of fresh leaves on the one hand, and newly flying sawdust on the other, cleared my head and made me feel part of the world again. I liked it so much I thought it was the best job I'd ever had—even though the hours were long and the wages rotten.

One day I saw an elderly man walking through the wood, followed by a little boy who ran in and out of the bushes whacking flowers with his stick. The kid was about four, dressed in cowboy suit and hat, the other hand firing off his six-shooter that made midget sharp cracks splitting like invisible twigs between the trees. He was pink-faced with grey eyes, the terror of cats and birds, a pest for the ice-cream man, the sort of kid half stunned by an avalanche of toys at Christmas, spoiled beyond recall by people with money. You could see it in his face.

I got a goz at the man, had to stare a bit before I saw it was Doris's father, the scrap merchant who'd not so long back been the menace of the street in his overdriven car. He was grey and wax in the face, well wrapped in topcoat and hat and scarf and treading carefully along the wood-path. "Come on," he said to the kid. "Come on, Tony, or you'll get lost."

I watched him run towards the old man, take his hand and say: "Are we going home now, grandad?" I had an impulse, which makes me blush to remember it, and that was to go up to Doris's ragman father and say—what I've already said in most of this story, to say that in a way he was my father as well, to say: "Hey up, dad. You don't know much, do you?" But I didn't, because I couldn't, leaned against a tree, feeling as if I'd done a week's work without stop, feeling a hundred years older than that old man who was walking off with my kid.

My last real sight of Doris was of her inside the shoe shop trying on shoes, and after that, when I switched off the light because I sensed danger, we both went into the dark, and never came out. But there's another and final picture of her that haunts me like a vision in my waking dreams. I see her coming down the street, all clean and golden-haired on that shining horse, riding it slowly towards our house to call on me, as she did for a long time. And she was known to men standing by the bookies as Lady Luck.

That's a long while ago, and I even see Doris's kid, a big lad now, running home from school. I can watch him without wanting to put my head in the gas oven, watch him and laugh to myself because I was happy to see him at all. He's in good hands and prospering. I'm going straight as well, working in the warehouse where they store butter and cheese. I eat like a fighting cock, and take home so much that my wife and two kids don't do bad on it either.

Noah's Ark*

While Jones the teacher unravelled the final meanderings of *Masterman Ready*, Colin from the classroom heard another trundle of wagons and caravans rolling slowly towards the open spaces of the Forest. His brain was a bottleneck, like the wide boulevard along which each vehicle passed, and he saw, remembering last year, fresh-packed ranks of colourful Dodgem Cars, traction engines and mobile zoos, Ghost Trains and Noah's Ark figures securely crated on to drays and lorries.

So *Masterman Ready* was beaten by the prospect of more tangible distraction, though it was rare for a book of dream-adventures to be banished so easily from Colin's mind. The sum total of such freelance wandering took him through bad days of scarcity, became a mechanical gaudily dressed pied-piper always ahead, which he would follow and one day scrag to see what made it tick. How this would come about he didn't know, didn't even try to find out—while the teacher droned on with the last few pages of his story.

Though his cousin Bert was eleven—a year older—Colin was already in a higher class at school, and felt that this counted for something anyway, even though he had found himself effortlessly there. With imagination fed by books to bursting point, he gave little thought to the rags he wore (except when it was cold) and face paradoxically overfleshed through lack of food. His hair was too short, even for a three-penny basin-crop at the barber's—which was the only thing that bothered him at school in that he was sometimes jocularly referred to as "Owd Bald-'ead".

*A round-about at the fair, so called because customers ride on a variety of wooden animals.

When the Goose Fair* came a few pennies had survived his weekly outlay on comics, but Bert had ways and means of spinning them far beyond their paltry value. "We'll get enough money for lots of rides," he said, meeting Colin at the street corner of a final Saturday. "I'll show you"—putting his arm around him as they walked up the street.

"How?" Colin wanted to know, protesting: "I'm not going to rob any shops. I'll tell you that now."

Bert, who had done such things, detected disapproval of his past, though sensing at the same time and with a certain pride that Colin would never have the nerve to crack open a shop at midnight and plug his black hands into huge jars of virgin sweets. "That's not the only way to get money," he scoffed. "You only do that when you want summat good. I'll show you what we'll do when we get there."

Along each misty street they went, aware at every turning of a low exciting noise from the northern sky. Bellies of cloud were lighted orange by the fair's reflection, plain for all to see, an intimidating bully slacking the will and drawing them towards its heart. "If it's on'y a penny a ride then we've got two goes each", Colin calculated with bent head, pondering along the blank flagstoned spaces of the pavement, hands in pockets pinning down his hard-begotten wealth. He was glad of its power to take him on to roundabouts, but the thought of what fourpence would do to the table at home filled him—when neither spoke—with spasms of deep misery. Fourpence would buy a loaf of bread or a bottle of milk or some stewing meat or a pot of jam or a pound of sugar. It would perhaps stop the agony his mother might be in from seeing his father black and brooding by the hearth if he—Colin—had handed the fourpence in for ten Woodbines from the corner shop. His father would take them with a smile, get up to kiss his mother in the fussy way he had and mash some tea, a happy man once more whose re-acquired asset would soon spread to everyone in the house.

It was marvellous what fourpence would do, if you were

*A very popular fair that is held in Nottingham every year. Geese used to be sold at it.

good enough to place it where it rightly belonged—which I'm not, he thought, because fourpence would also buy a fistful of comics, or two bars of chocolate or take you twice to the flea-pit picture-house or give you four rides on Goose Fair, and the division, the wide dark soil-smelling trench that parted good from bad was filled with wounds of unhappiness. And such unhappiness was suspect, because Colin knew that whistling stone-throwing Bert at his side wouldn't put up with it for the mere sake of fourpence—no, he'd spend it and enjoy it, which he was now out to do with half the pennies Colin had. If Bert robbed a shop or cart he'd take the food straight home—that much Colin knew—and if he laid his hands on five bob or a pound he'd give his mother one and six and say that that was all he'd been able to get doing some sort of work. But fourpence wouldn't worry him a bit. He'd just enjoy it. And so would Colin, except in the space of stillness between roundabouts.

They were close to the fair, walking down the slope of Bentinck Road, able to distinguish between smells of fish-and-chips, mussels and brandysnap. "Look on the floor." Bert called out, ever-sharp and hollow-cheeked with the fire of keeping himself going, lit by an instinct never to starve yet always looking as if he were starving. The top and back of his head was padded by overgrown hair, and he slopped along in broken slippers, hands in pockets, whistling, then swearing black and blue at being swept off the pavement by a tide of youths and girls.

Colin needed little telling: snapped down to the gutter, walked a hundred yards doubled-up like a premature rheumatic, and later shot straight holding a packet with two whole cigarettes protruding. "No whacks!" he cried, meaning: No sharing.

"Come on," Bert said, cajoling, threatening, "don't be bleedin'-well mingy, our Colin. Let's 'ave one."

Colin stood firm. Finding was keeping. "I'm savin' 'em for our dad. I don't suppose 'e's got a fag to 'is name."

"Well, my old man ain't never got no fags either, but I wun't bother to save 'em for 'im if I found any. I mean it as well."

"P'raps we'll have a drag later on then," Colin conceded, keeping them in his pocket. They were on the asphalt path of the Forest, ascending a steep slope. Bert feverishly ripped open every cast-down packet now, chucking silver paper to the wind, slipping picture-cards in his pocket for younger brothers, crushing what remained into a ball and hurling it towards the darkness where bodies lay huddled together in some passion that neither of them could understand or even remotely see the point of.

From the war memorial they viewed the whole fair, a sea of lights and tent tops flanked on two sides by dimly shaped houses whose occupants would be happy when the vast encampment scattered the following week to other towns. A soughing groan of pleasure was being squeezed out of the earth, and an occasional crescendo of squeals reached them from the Swingboats and Big Wheel as though an army were below, offering human sacrifices before beginning its march. "Let's get down there," Colin said, impatiently turning over his pennies. "I want to see things. I want to get on that Noah's Ark."

Sucking penny sticks of brandysnap they pushed by the Ghost Train, hearing girls screaming from its skeleton-filled bowels. "We'll roll pennies on to numbers and win summat," Bert said. "It's easy, you see. All you've got to do is put the pennies on a number when the woman ain't looking." He spoke eagerly, to get Colin's backing in a project that would seem more of an adventure if they were in it together. Not that he was afraid to cheat alone, but suspicion rarely fell so speedily on a pair as it did on a lone boy obviously out for what his hands could pick up. "It's dangerous," Colin argued, though all but convinced, elbowing his way behind. "You'll get copped."

A tall gipsy-looking woman with black hair done up in a ponytail stood in the penny-a-roll stall, queen of its inner circle. She stared emptily before her, though Colin, edging close, sensed how little she missed of movement round about. A stack of coppers crashed regularly from one hand to the other, making a noise which, though not loud, drew attention to the stall—and the woman broke its rhythm now and again to issue with an expression of absolute impartiality a few coins to a nick-hatted man who by controlling two of the wooden slots managed to roll down four pennies at a time. "He ain't winnin', though," Bert whispered in Colin's ear, who saw the truth of it: that he rolled out more than he picked up.

His remark stung through to the man's competing brain. "Who ain't?" he demanded, letting another half-dozen pennies go before swinging round on him.

"Yo' ain't", Bert chelped.

"Ain't I?"—swung-open mac showing egg and beer stains around his buttons.

Bert stood his ground, blue eyes staring. "No, y'ain't."

"That's what yo' think," the man retorted, in spite of everything, even when the woman scooped up more of his pennies.

Bert pointed truculently. "Do you call that winning then? Look at it. I don't." All eyes met on three sad coins lying between squares, and Bert slipped his hand on to the counter where the man had set down a supply-dump of money. Colin watched, couldn't breathe, from fear but also from surprise even though there was nothing about Bert he did not know. A shilling and a sixpence seemed to run into Bert's palm, were straightaway hidden by black fingers curling over them. He reached a couple of pennies with the other hand, but his wrist became solidly clamped against the board. He cried out: "Oo, yer rotten sod. Yer'r 'urtin' me."

The man's eyes, formerly nebulous with beer, now became deep and self-centred with righteous anger. "You should keep your thievin' fingers to yoursen. Come on, you little bogger, drop them pennies."

Colin felt ashamed and hoped he would, wanted to get it over with and lose himself among spinning roundabouts. The black rose of Bert's hand unfolded under pressure, petal by petal, until the coins slid off. "Them's my pennies," he complained. "It's yo' as is the thief, not me. You're a bully as well. I had 'em there ready to roll down as soon as I could get one of them slot things."

"I was looking the other way," said the woman, avoiding trouble; which made the man indignant at getting no help: "Do you think I'm daft then? And blind as well?" he cried.

"You must be," Bert said quietly, "if you're trying to say I nicked your money." Colin felt obliged to back him up: "He didn't pinch owt," he said earnestly, exploiting a look of honesty he could put at will into his face. "I'm not his pal, mate, but I'll tell you the truth. I was just passin' an' stopped to look, and he put tuppence down on there, took it from 'is own pocket."

"You thievin' Radford lot," the man responded angrily, though freed now from the dead-end of continual losing. "Get cracking from here, or I'll call a copper."

Bert wouldn't move. "Not till you've gen me my tuppence back. I worked 'ard for that, at our dad's garden, diggin' taters up and weedin'." The woman looked vacantly—sending a column of pennies from one palm to another—beyond them into packed masses swirling and pushing around her flimsy island. With face dead-set in dreadful purpose, hat tilted forward and arms all-embracing what money was his, the man gave in to his fate of being a loser and scooped up all his coins, though he was struck enough in conscience to leave Bert two surviving pennies before making off to better luck at another stall.

"That got shut on 'im," Bert said, his wink at Colin meaning they were one and eightpence to the good.

The riches lasted for an hour, and Colin couldn't remember having been partner to so much capital, wanted to guard some from the avid tentacles of the thousand-lighted fair. But it fled from their itchy fingers—surrendered or captured, it was hard to say which—spent on shrimps and candyfloss, cakewalk and helter-skelter. They pushed by sideshow fronts. "You should have saved some of that dough," Colin said, unable to get used to being poor again.

"It's no use savin' owt," Bert said. "If you spend it you can allus get some more"—and became paralysed at the sight of a half-dressed woman in African costume standing by a paybox with a python curled around her buxom top.

Colin argued: "If you save you get money and you can go away to Australia or China. I want to go to foreign countries. Eh", he said with a nudge, "it's a wonder that snake don't bite her, ain't it?"

Bert laughed. "It's the sort that squeezes yer ter death, but they gi' 'em pills to mek 'em dozy. I want to see foreign countries as well, but I'll join the army."

"That's no good," Colin said, leading the way to more roundabouts, "there'll be a war soon, and you might get killed." Around the base of a Noah's Ark Bert discovered a tiny door that let them into a space underneath. Colin looked in, to a deadly midnight noise of grinding machinery. "Where yer going?"

But Bert was already by the middle, doubled up to avoid the flying circular up-and-down world rolling round at full speed above. It seemed to Colin the height of danger—one blow, or get up without thinking, and you'd be dead, brains smashed into grey sand, which would put paid to any thoughts of Australia. Bert though had a cool and accurate sense of proportion, which drew Colin in despite his fear. He crawled on hands and knees, until he came level with Bert and roared into his ear: "What yer looking for?"

"Pennies," Bert screamed back above the din.

They found nothing, retired to a more simple life among the crowd. Both were hungry, and Colin told himself it must have been five hours since his four o'clock tea. "I could scoff a hoss between two mattresses."

"So could I," Bert agreed. "But look what I'm going to do." A white-scarfed youth wearing a cap, with a girl on his arm working her way through an outsize candyfloss, emerged from a gap in the crowd. Colin saw Bert go up to them and say a few words to the youth, who put his hand in his pocket, made a joke that drew a laugh from the girl, and gave something to Bert.

"What yer got?" Colin demanded when he came back.

Ingenious Bert showed him. "A penny. I just went up and said I was hungry and asked 'im for summat."

"I'll try," Colin said, wanting to contribute his share. Bert pulled him back, for the only people available were a middle-aged man and his wife, well-dressed and married. "They wain't gi' yer owt. You want to ask courting couples, or people on their own."

But the man on his own whom Colin asked was argumentative. A penny was a penny. Two and a half cigarettes. "What do you want it for?"

"I'm hungry," was all Colin could say.

A dry laugh. "So am I."

"Well, I'm hungrier. I ain't 'ad a bite t' eat since this morning, honest." The man hesitated, but fetched a handful of coins from his pocket. "You'd better not let a copper see you begging or you'll get sent to borstal."

Some time later they counted out a dozen pennies. "You don't get nowt unless you ask, as mam allus tells me," Bert grinned. They stood at a tea stall with full cups and a plate of buns, filling themselves to the brim. The nearby Big Wheel spun its passengers towards the clouds, only to spin them down again after a tantalizing glimpse of the whole fair, each descending girl cutting the air with animal screams that made Colin shudder until he realized that they were in no harm, were in fact probably enjoying it. "I feel better now," he said, putting his cup back on the counter.

They walked around caravans backed on to railings at the Forest edge, looked up steps and into doorways, at bunks and potbellied stoves, at beautiful closed doors painted in many colours and carved with weird designs that mystified Colin and made him think of the visit once made to the Empire. Gipsies, Goose Fair, Theatre—it was all one to him, a heaven-on-earth because together they made up the one slender bridge-head of another world that breached the tall thickets surrounding his own. A connecting link between them was in the wild-eyed children now and again seated on wooden steps; but when Colin went too near for a closer look a child called out in alarm, and a burly adult burst from the caravan and chased them away.

Colin took Bert's arm as they wedged themselves into the solid mass of people, under smoke of food-stalls and traction engines, betweeen lit-up umbrellas and lights on poles. "We've spent all our dough," he said, "and don't have owt left to go on Noah's Ark wi'."

"You don't ev ter worry about that. All yer got ter do is get on and keep moving from one thing to another, following the man collecting the cash so's he never sees yer or catches up wi' yer. Got me?"

Colin didn't like the sound of it, but went up the Noah's Ark steps, barging through lines of onlookers. "I'll do it first", Bert said. "So keep yer eyes on me and see how it's done. Then yo' can go on."

He first of all straddled a lion. Colin stood by the rail and watched closely. When the Ark began spinning Bert moved discreetly to a cock just behind the attendant who emerged from a hut-like structure in the middle. The roundabout soon took on its fullest speed, until Colin could hardly distinguish one animal from another, and often lost sight of Bert in the quick-roaring spin.

Then the world stopped circling, and his turn came: "Are you staying on for a second go?" Bert said no, that it wasn't wise to do it two times on the trot. Colin well knew that it was wrong, and dangerous, which was more to the point, yet when a Noah's Ark stood in your path spinning with the battle honours of its more than human speed-power written on the face of each brief-glimpsed wooden animal, you had by any means to get yourself on to that platform, money or no money, fear or no fear, and stay there through its violent bucking until it stopped. Watching from the outside it seemed that one ride on the glorious Noah's Ark would fill you with similar inexhaustible energy for another year, that at the end of the ride you wouldn't want to come off, would need to stay on for ever until you were either sick or dead with hunger.

He was riding alone, clinging to a tiger on the outer ring of vehicles, slightly sick with apprehension and at the sudden up-and-down motion of starting. He waved to Bert on the first slow time round. Then the roundabout's speed increased and it was necessary to stop hugging the tiger and follow the attendant who had just emerged to begin collecting the fares. But he was afraid, for it seemed that should only one of his fingers relax its hold he would be shot off what was suppose to be a delicious ride and smashed to pieces on hitting the outside rail—or smash anyone else to pieces who happened to be leaning against it.

However, with great effort and a sinking heart he leapt: panic jettisoned only in the space between two animals. In this state he almost derailed a near-by couple, and when the man's hand shot out for revenge he felt the wind of a near miss blowing by the side of his face. The vindictive fist continued to ply even when he was securely seated on a zebra so that, faced with more solid danger than empty space, he put his tongue out at the man and let go once more.

He went further forward, still in sight of the attendant's stooping enquiring back. In his confused zig-zag progress—for few animals were now vacant—he worked inward to the centre where it was safer, under a roof of banging drums and cymbals, thinking at one point to wave victoriously to Bert. But the idea slipped over a cliff as he threw himself forward and held on to a horse's tail.

The roundabout could go on faster, judging by shouts and squeals from the girls. Colin's movements were clumsy, and he envied the attendant's dexterity a few yards in front, and admired Bert who had made this same circular Odyssey with so much aplomb. Aware of peril every second he was more fretful now of being shot like a cannonball against wood and iron than being caught by the money-collector. "Bogger this," he cursed. "I don't like it a bit"—laughing grimly and lunging out on a downgrade, pegged by even more speed to a double-seated dragon.

A vacant crocodile gave a few seconds enjoyment before he leapt on to an ant-eater to keep his distance equal from the attendant. He thought his round should have finished by now, but suddenly the man turned and began coming back, looking at each rider to be sure they had paid. This was unprecedented. They weren't lax, but once round in one direction was all they ever did—so Bert had assured him—and now here was this sly rotten bastard who'd got the cheek to come round again. That worn't fair.

The soporific, agreeable summer afternoons of *Masterman*

Ready, having laid a trap at the back of his mind, caught him for a moment, yet flew away unreal before this real jungle in which he had somehow stumbed. He had to move back now in full view of the attendant, to face a further apprenticeship at taking the roundabout clockwise. It seemed impossible, and in one rash moment he considered making a flying leap into the solid stationary gangway and getting right out of it—for he was certain the man had marked him down, was out to wring his neck before pitching the dead chicken that remained over the heads of the crowd. He glimpsed him, an overalled greasy bastard whose lips clung to a doused-out nub-end, cashbag heavy but feet sure.

How long's this bleeding ride going to go on? he asked himself. It's been an hour already and Bert swore blind it only lasted three minutes. I thought so as well, but I suppose they're making it longer just because that bloke's after me for having cadged a free ride. This jungle was little different from home and street life, yet alarming, more frightening because the speed was exaggerated. His one thought was to abandon the present jungle, hurl himself into the slower with which he was familiar—though in that also he felt a dragging pain that would fling him forth one day.

He went back the same way, almost feeling an affection now on coming against a muzzle, ear or tail he'd already held on to, going from the sanctuary of ant-eater to dragon to crocodile slowly, then gathering speed and surety in leaping from horse to zebra to tiger and back to lion and cock. No rest for the wicked his mother always said. But I'm not wicked, he told himself. You'll still get no rest though. I don't want any rest. Not much you don't. Clear-headed now, he was almost running with the roundabout, glancing back when he could—to see the attendant gaining on him—dodging irate fists that lashed out when he missed his grip and smiling at enraged astonished faces as if nothing were the matter, holding on to coat-tail and animal that didn't belong to him.

Things never turn out right, he swore, never, never. Rank-a-tank-a-tank-tank went the music. Clash-ter-clash-ter-clash-clash flew the cymbals, up and down to squeals and shouts, and bump-bump-bump-bumpity-bump went his heart, still audible above everything else, lashing out at the insides of his ears with enormous boxing-gloves, throttling his windpipe with a cloven hoof, stumping on his stomach as though he were a tent from which ten buck-navvies were trying to escape, wanting a pint after a week of thirst.

A hand slid over his shoulder, but with a violent twist he broke free and continued his mad career around the swirling Ark. "He'll get me, he'll get me. He's a man and can run faster than I can. He's had more practice than me." But he lurched and righted himself, spurted forward as if in a race, making such progress that he saw the man's back before him, instead of fleeing from his reaching hand behind. He slowed down too late, for the man, evidently controlled by a wink from the centre, switched back. Colin swivelled also, on the run again.

Compared to what it had been the speed now appeared a snail's pace. The three-minute ride was almost up, but Colin, thinking he would escape, was caught, more securely this time, by neck-scruff and waist. He turned within the grasp, smelling oil and sweat and tobacco, pulling and striking at first then, on an inspired impulse kicking wildly at his ankle, unaware of the pain he was causing because of stabbing aches that spread over his own stubbed toes. The man swore as proficiently as Colin's father when he hit his thumb once putting up shelves in the kitchen. But he was free, and considered that the roundabout, up-and-down-about was going slow enough to make a getaway. No need to wait until it really stops, was his last thought.

It was like Buck Rogers landing from a space ship without due care, though a few minutes passed before he was able to think this. Upon leaving the still-swirling platform his body fell into a roll and went out with some force, crashing like a sensitive flesh-and-bone cannonball between a courting couple and piling against the wooden barrier. The ball his body made without him knowing much about it slewed out when he hit the posts, arms and legs flying against the carved and painted woodwork of the balustrade. Clump-

clump—in quick succession—but he wasn't aware of any standstill either beyond or behind his soon-opened eyes. The rank-a-tank-tank-tank played him out, a blurring of red-white-and-blue lights and coloured animals, and a feeling of relief once he was away from his pursuer, no matter what peril the reaching of solid earth might surround him with.

Bert had watched the whole three minutes, had tried pushing a way through the crowd to catch Colin as he came off—a small ragged figure elbowing a passage between lounging semi-relaxed legs that nevertheless were not always easy to move, so that he reached him late. "Come on," he said in a worried voice, "gerrup. I'll give yer a hand. Did yer enjoy your ride?"—trying to make him stand up. Turning to an enquirer: "No, he's my cousin, and he's all right. I can tek care on 'im. Come on, Colin. He's still after you, so let's blow."

Colin's legs were rubber, wanted to stay against the sympathetic hardness of wood. "He slung me off after speeding it up, the rotten sod. It was a dirty trick."

"Come on," Bert urged. "Let's blow town."

"Leave me. I'll crawl. I'll kill him if he comes near me." No spinning now: he felt floorboards, saw legs and the occasional flash of a passing wooden animal. They'd started up again. "It's your turn now, ain't it?" he said angrily to Bert.

No time was lost. Bert bent down and came up with him on his shoulders like an expert gymnast, going white in the face and tottering down the wooden steps, towards warm soil and dust. On the last step he lost his strength, swerved helplessly to the right, and both donkey and burden crashed out of sight by the bottom roundabout boards where no one went.

They lay where they had fallen. "I'm sorry," Bert said. "I didn't know he was looking out for us. And then you go and cop it. A real bastard." His hand was under Colin's armpit to stop him sliding sideways. "Are you all right, though? I wun't a minded if it 'ad bin me, and I mean it. Do you feel sick? Are you going to spew?"—hand clapped over Colin's mouth, that was closed tight anyway. "The snakey bastard, chasing you off like that. He ought to get summonsed, he did an' all."

Colin suddenly stood up, leaned against the boards and, with more confidence in his legs, staggered into the crowd, followed by Bert. Abject and beaten, they walked around until midnight by which time, both dead-tired, the idea occurred to them of going home. "I'll get pasted," Colin said, "because I'm supposed to be in by ten." Bert complained that he was knackered, that he wanted to get back anyway.

Streets around the fair were shrivelling into darkness, took on the hue of cold damp ash. They walked arm-in-arm, inspired enough by empty space to sing loudly a song that Bert's father had taught him:

We don't want to charge with the fusiliers
Bomb with the bombardiers
Fight for the racketeers
We want to stay at home!
We want to stay at home!
We want to stay at home!

words ringing loud and clear out of two gruff voices slopping along on sandalled feet, mouths wide open and arms on each other's shoulders turning corners and negotiating twitchells, singing twice as loud by dead cinema and damp graveyard:

We don't want to fight in a Tory war
Die like the lads before
Drown in the mud and gore
We want to go to work. . . .

swinging along from one verse to another, whose parrot-fashioned words were less important than the bellows of steamy breath fogging up cold air always in front of them, frightening cats and skirting midnight prowlers, and hearing people tell them to shurrup and let them sleep from angrily rattled bedroom windows. They stood in the middle of a bigger road when a car was coming, rock still to test their nerves by making it stop, then charging off when they had been successful, to avoid the driver's rage, to reach another corner and resume locked arms, swinging along to the tune of Rule Britannia:

Rule two tanners
Two tanners make a bob,
King George nevernevernever
SHAVES HIS NOB!

each note wavering on the air, and dying as they turned a corner; at least it would have sounded like that, if anyone had been listening to it from the deserted corner before. But to Colin, the noise stayed, all around their heads and faces, grinding away the sight and sound of the Noah's Ark jungle he had ridden on free, and so been pitched from.

The Firebug

I smile as much as feel ashamed at the memory of some of the things I did when I was a lad, even though I caused my mother a lot of trouble. I used to pinch her matches and set fire to heaps of paper and anything I could get my eyes on.

I was no bigger than sixpenorth o' coppers, so's you'd think I wasn't capable of harming a fly. People came straight out with it: "Poor little bogger. Butter wouldn't melt in his mouth." But my auntie used to say: "He might not be so daft as he looks when he grows up"—and she was right, I can see that now. Her husband had a few brains as well: "He's quiet, nobody can deny it, but still waters run deep. I wouldn't trust him an inch." At this the rest of the family got on to him and called him bully with neither sense or feeling, said I was delicate and might not have long for this world—while, I went on eating my way through a fistful of bread-and-jam as if I hadn't heard a dickybird and would last forever.

This match craze must have started when, still in leggings, I was traipsed downtown by my mother one day midweek. The streets weren't all that crowded and I held on to her carrier-bag, dragging a bit I should think, slurring my other hand along the cold glass of shop windows full of tricycles and forts for Christmas that I would never get—unless they were given to me as a reward for being good enough not to pinch 'em. As usual my mother was harassed to death (on her way to ask for a bit more time to pay off the arrears of 24 Slum Yard I shouldn't wonder) and I was grizzling because I couldn't share as much as I'd have liked in the razzle-dazzle of the downtown street.

Suddenly I left off moaning, felt the air go quiet and

blue, as if a streak of sly lightning had stiffened everybody dead in their tracks. Even motor cars stopped. "What's up, mam?" I said—or whined I expect, because I could only whine up to fourteen: then I went to work and started talking clear and proper, from shock.

Before she could tell me, a bloody great bell began clanging—louder than any school or church call—bowling its ding-dong from every place at once, so that I looked quickly at the up-windows to wonder where it was coming from. I felt myself going white, knees quaking. Not that I was terrified. I was right in the middle of another world, as if the one and only door to it had a bell on saying PRESS, and somebody was leaning his elbow spot-on and drilling right into my startled brain.

The bells got louder, so's I couldn't any longer hope it was only the cops or an ambulance. It was something I'd never seen before nor dreamt of either: a flying red-faced monster batting along the narrow street at a flat-out sixty, as if it had been thrown there like a toy. Only this weighed a ton or two and made the ground shake under me, like a procession for the Coronation or something—but coming at top speed, as if a couple of Russian tanks were after its guts and shooting fire behind. "What is it, mam? What is it?" I whined when it got quiet enough to speak.

"Only a fire," she told me. "A house is on fire, and they're fire-engines going to put it out." Then another couple of engines came belting through the deadened street, both together it seemed turning all the air into terrifying klaxons. I started screaming, and didn't stop until I'd gone down in a fit.

Mam and a man carried me into the nearest shop and when I woke up there was nothing but toys all around, so's I thought I was in heaven. To keep me calm the shop-keeper gave me a lead soldier which I was glad to grab, though I'd rather have had the toy fire-engine that caught at my sight as soon as I stood up. It was as if my eyes had opened for the first time since I was born: red with yellow ladders and blue men in helmets—but he turned me away to ask if I was all right, and when I nodded walked me back into the street out of temptation. I was a bit of a bogger in them days.

The long school holidays of summer seemed to go on for years. When I could scrounge fourpence I'd nip to the continuous downtown pictures after dinner and drop myself in one of the front seats, to see the same film over and over till driven out by hunger or God save the king. But I didn't often get money to go, and now and again mam would bundle me into the street so's her nerves could have a rest from my "give-me-this-and-I-want-that" sort of grizzling. I'd be quite happy—after the shock of being slung out had worn off—to sit on the pavement making wrinkles in the hot tar with a spoon I'd managed to grab on my way through the kitchen, or drawing patterns with a piece of slate or matchstick. Other kids would be rolling marbles or running at rounders, or a string of them would scream out of an entry after playing hide and seek in somebody's backyard. A few would be away at seaside camp, or out in the fields and woods on Sunday treats, so it worn't as noisy as it might have been. I remember once I sat dead quiet all afternoon doing nothing but talk to myself for minutes at a time on what had happened to me in the last day or two and about things I hoped to do as soon as I got either money or matches in my fist—chuntering ten to the dozen as if somebody unknown to me had put a penny in the gramophone of my brain as they walked by. Other people passing looked at me gone-out, but I didn't give a bogger and just went on talking until the noise of a fire-engine in the distance came through to my locked-in world.

It sounded like a gale just starting up, an aeroplane of bells going along at ground level with folded wings, about ten streets off but far enough away to seem as if it was in another town behind the big white clouds of summer, circling round a dream I'd had about a fire a few nights ago. It didn't sound real, though I knew what it meant now, after my downtown fit a long time back in the winter. Hot sun and empty sky stopped it being loud I suppose, but my heart nearly fell over itself at the brass-band rattle, it went so fast—sitting in my mouth like a cough-drop or dollymixture getting bigger as the bells went on. Most of the other kids ran hollering to where the noise came from, even when I thought they were too far off for anybody else to hear, went clobbering up the street and round the corner until everywhere was quiet and empty except the bells now reaching louder all the time.

I wanted to join in the chase, fly towards fire and smoke as fast as my oversize wellingtons would take me, to see all them helmeted men with hatchets and ladders and hosepipes trying to stop the red flames but not managing so that the only thing left was a couple of cinders one on top of the other. And then I'd try to sneak up and blow the top one off. But I'd never be able to catch them, that much I knew as sure as God made little apples, so I waited till my face changed back from white to mucky and my blood stopped bumping and went on playing tar games in the sun.

But sometimes I'd sit and hear the bells of a fire engine that none of the other kids would hear, would leave off playing and listen hard for it to come closer, hoping to see one swivel around the bend at the top of our street and pour down with its big nose getting closer—and if it did I wouldn't know whether to stick by and see what happened or run screaming in to mam and get her to hide me under the stairs. I was always hoping for a sweltering fire close by so that I could watch them trying to put it out—hope for one at the bike factory or pub or in some shop or other. But I just heard them now and again in my mind, sat (before I cottoned on to this) waiting for the others to hear it and run yelling to where it come from, but they didn't and then I knew it was just in me the bells had played. This was only on summer days though, as if the sun melted wax in my tabs and let me hear better than anybody else—even things that didn't happen at all.

But fire-engine fires were rare as five-pound notes, and up to then the nearest a big blaze ever came to our street was on Bonfire Night. They told us about Bonfire Night at school, about how this poor bloke Guy Fawkes got chucked on a fire because he wanted to blow up parliament, and I learned as well about the Great Fire of London where all the town got lit because everything was built of wood. What a sight that must have been! Thousands and thousands of houses going up like matchboxes. Still, I didn't like to think of people getting burnt to death, I do know that. I was terrified on it, and so was dad, and though he used to poke the fire cold out every night, and pull the rugs a long way back from the grate and set the chairs under the window, I was still worried in bed later in case a hot coal lit up again and walked to right across the room where the rugs were; on that somebody next door would go to sleep with his pipe lit and the first thing I'd know was a rubber hose slooshing water through the window and onto us four kids. I wouldn't even have heard the ding-dong-belling of the fire-engine I slept so deep—and that would have broken my heart.

On Bonfire Night fires were lit like cherry trees, two or three to a long street like ours, and the only thing I ever prayed for was that it wouldn't rain after the bigger lads got busy and set their matches under piles of mattresses, boxes and old sofas. The flames climbed so high by ten that house walls glowed and shone as if somebody had scrubbed them clean, and I used to go from one fire-hill to another eating my bread and jam and jumping out of the way when firecrackers got close. I was so excited the bread almost wouldn't go down, and my breath gulped as the warmth tried to ram itself through my throat when I went too near the fire.

If only flames like this blazed all winter, was my one big wish. But they didn't, my brain told me: they flared for one night, hands of fire waving hello and good-bye while we shouted and danced, then died to a glowing hump of grey ash for corporation carts to clear away like the bodies of big runover dogs next morning. Christmas was a let-down after these mountainous fires.

This Bonfire Night I stayed out till twelve hoping, now that everybody else had gone, for a last-minute flame to shoot up for one second and show its face only to me; but all that remained was the smell of fire-ash and gunpowder. Then in the dead quietness I heard the bell of a far-off fire-engine, flying down some empty street with bells full on, passing houses that were so quiet you might think God had gone before and like some fat publican shouted TIME in each. I looked at the fire again in the hope that it would flare and bring the distant engine to where I was, frightened a bit at the same time because I was on my own and would have nobody to stand with if it did. All I got for my waiting though was a spot of ice-cold rain on my arm, and the sound of another big drop burying itself with a hiss chock in the middle of the ash. And the fire-engine went tingling on till I couldn't hear it no more, off to some street where, I thought, they had a bigger fire then could ever be built in ours.

My first fires were nothing to speak of: baby ones built in the backyard with a single sheet of paper that burned out in half a second like celluloid, scattering like black butterflies at the draught of another kid. Mam clouted my tab-hole and took the matches off me—to begin with—but realising after a while how it kept me occupied at a time when she was hard-up for peace and quiet she let me play: a couple of old newspapers and half a dozen matches stopped me whining for an hour, which was cheap at the price. For mam was badly right enough, holding her heart all the time and blue in the face when anything harassed her, so that even if I'd wanted to make a row dad would have thumped me one.

So nobody bothered me and my midget fires, because they could see I wasn't doing no harm. One or two of the nosey parkers went as far as to tut-tut loud when they looked over the fence in passing and saw wisps of smoke floating in front of my eyes, but they soon got used to the sight of it and stopped pulling meagrims. They must have known mam knew I'd got the matches, and didn't want a row with her because she was still a wild fighter badly or not. I soon stopped making fires outside our back door, though, because one day I collected a whole tin of matchsticks off the street and they burnt so long in a bad wind that when mam smelled them up in the bedroom dad kicked the fire out with his boots and locked the gate on me. I'd only got a couple o' matches left, and had forgotten to snatch up the newspaper then dad's fist lifted me, so I was feeling hard done by as I sulked near the yard lavatories.

At the first nip of a cold rainspot I went into the nearest because if there was one thing I didn't like it was getting wet. It made me feel so miserable I could have put my head in the gas-oven or gone to the railway line and played with an express till I was bumped into, rolled over, and blacked-out for good. Whenever a spot of rain fell I sheltered in a shop doorway or entry until it stopped even if I was there for hours, because when rain landed on me it was like a shock of pins and needles sending me off my nut, as if every bit of me was a funny bone. And big rain was worse than ever, for it seemed to stick into me like falling penknives.

If I hadn't opened the door and gone in to get out of the rain I'd never have noticed the wad of newspapers stuffed behind the lavatory pipe. Two or three thick Sunday ones, the sort I liked because they'd got bigger letters on the front page than any. Once at Aunt Ethel's one of my grown-up cousins was reading the Sunday paper and his brother put a light to the bottom for a lark, and the other didn't know what was going off till flames reached the terrible headlines and started licking his nose. Or maybe he did, for he stayed as calm as if it had happened before: he was near the range and when the whole paper was in flames just leaned over and let it fall in the firegrate to burn itself out—as if he'd read all he wanted to anyway—and calmly asked his mam if there was any more tea in the pot. I laughed at the thought of it for days and days.

As soon as the heap of papers caught I ran out of the yard and rattled to the bottom of the street, went up to a gang of pals and played marbles so's nobody'd twig anything. I was so excited at what I'd done, and at listening all the time for a fire-engine (that I hoped somebody had called to come rumbling full tilt down the cobbled street with bells ringing), that I lost all my five marbles because I hardly knew what I was doing.

I didn't hear the bells of a fire-engine though: the only

ringing that went on was all night in my ears after the old man had given me a good pasting when I went home a long time later. The whole yard talked about my fire-making for days: "The little varmint wants taming. He's got too much on it."

"You'd better lock your door when you go over the road shopping, or he might sneak in and send your home up in flames."

"If I was his mother I'd take him to have his brains tested, though she can't do a sight at the moment, poor woman. So he gets neglected. I don't know, I don't."

"He'd be better off at Cumberland Hall," another woman said—which made me shiver when I heard it because Cumberland Hall's a stark cold place they send kids to as ain't got no mam and dad, where they hit you with sticks, feed you on bread and porridge, and get you up at six in the morning—or so mam once told me when I asked her about it. And it was a long way in the woods, she said, so's I knew if I got sent there I wouldn't be able to hear a fire-engine for years and years. Unless I made a fire on the sly and one had to come and put it out, then I might, but you couldn't depend on it because I knew by now that fire-engines didn't fly ding-donging to every bit of fire in the open air: they had to be big ones, which meant I was beginning to learn. Also I didn't want to get caught again and have my head batted, for as well as it hurting a long time afterwards it might send me daft or dead which would be terrible because then I wouldn't be able to make the fires or hear the engines.

So I knew I'd got to be careful next time and thought about how secret you could be if you did it in a wood and how big a fire it'd grow to if once it got going and the wind blew on it. I dreamed about it for weeks, saw yellow match-light jump to paper, spread to dry leaves and twigs, climb to dead wood and branches and bushes and little trees and big trees, changing colour from red to blue and green and back to red as the big bell ding-donged through everything, racing from the main road. And all the firemen would just stand there, helmets off and scratching their heads because they wouldn't have a dog's chance of putting it out. I was sweating myself at the thought of it. Once on the pictures I saw where a big oil well caught fire, and they had to have dynamite to put it out. Dynamite! Think of that! Many's the pasting I got from the teacher at school for being half asleep in these daydreams. Once I was called out to the front for it, and as he was holding the strap up to let me have it, the thundery quiet of the classroom was filled with the roar of a fire-engine out on the boulevard. A few seconds went by as everybody wondered where it was going, and I thought the teacher would let me off at such a fire-awful noise, (though I don't know why he should), but the next thing I knew the strap had hit the outstretched palm of my hand as if a large stone had fallen on it from a thousand feet up. The bastard. I should have been listening to him telling us about how the army of some batchy king or other chopped up the senseless blokes of another army; then the two kings shook hands and signed a bit of paper to say things should be the same, but peaceful, and all the soldiers just sat in gangs around their little fires boiling soup and laughing, when all I thought of was how all these little fires could be joined together into a big blaze, as big as a mountain, with the two kings on top instead of that poor bloke called Guy Fawkes—just because he had a funny name.

I went off early one morning, a sunny day one Sunday, all by myself after a breakfast of tomatoes and bacon. Dad was glad to get rid of me because mam was still badly and the doctor was up with her. She hadn't spoken to me for a week because she'd been sleeping most of the time—and all I had to do, dad said, was keep out of her way and then she'd get better quicker.

Well, I was glad to because I'd got other things to brood on, walking down the street well into the wall with a box of matches and some folded paper in my pockets, my hand clutching the matches because I didn't want them to jump out—or fall through the hole that might get wider as I walked along. I'd be hard put to it to get any more if they did, because I hadn't got a penny to my name. Admitted, I could always stop and ask people to give me a match, but it was risky, because I'd often tried it, though sometimes I managed to beg one or two from a bloke who didn't care what I was up to and perhaps wanted me to smoke myself to death, or set Nottingham on fire. But mostly the people I asked either pushed me away and said clear off, or told me they were sorry but their matches were safeties and no good without a box. Now and again a bloke with safeties would give me a few anyway—wanting to help me and hoping I'd find some way to strike them, though I never did, unless I lit them with proper matches I latched on to later. The people I never asked were women, after the first one or two had threatened to fetch a copper, being clever enough to twig what I was up to.

Wind blew my hair about as I crossed the railway bridge by the station. Trolley buses trundled both ways and mostly empty, though even if I'd had a penny I'd still have walked, for walking my legs off made me feel I was going somewhere, strolling along though not too slow and enjoying the faces of fresh air that met me by the time I got out to the open spaces of Western Boulevard. I was feeling free and easy, and hoped a copper wouldn't stop me and ask what I was doing with paper and matches sticking out of my pockets. But nobody bothered me and I turned down from the bridge and onto the canal bank, looking in deep locks now and again, at the endless bottoms of water, as if the steep sides of the smooth wall still went on underneath—to the middle of the earth as far as I knew. A funny thought came to me: how long would it take for this canyon with water at the bottom to be filled to the brim with the fine and flimsy ash from cigarettes, only that? I sat on a lock gate and wondered: how many people need to smoke how many fags for how many years? Donkey's years, I supposed. I'd be an old man on two sticks by then. Even teachers at school wouldn't be able to work that sum out. I stood up and had a long pee down into the smooth surface, my pasty face in the mirror of it shivered to bits when the first piss struck.

After a good while of more walking I cut off along a lane at the next bridge leading towards the wood I'd set my heart on: a toy for Christmas. I was excited, already heard fire-engines crossing the sky, bells going off miles away, a sound that thrilled me even though I did know I was hearing things. The wheat was tall, yellow and dusty-looking over hedges and gates bushes so high along the lane that sometimes I couldn't see the sky. Faded fag packets and scorched newspaper had been thrown among nettles and scrub by lads and courting couples out from Nottingham, for the fields weren't all that far off from the black and smother-cating streets. My teeth still felt funny at the screams of tree-trunks from Sunday overtime at the sawmill not far off, though after a while I couldn't hear anything at all, except the odd thrush or blackbird nipping about like bats trying to get their own shadows in their beaks. I'd been out here a time or two with pals looking for eggs in birds' nets but I wasn't interested in that any more because my uncle once caught me with some and told me it was wicked and wrong to rob birds of their young 'uns.

So I walked by the hedge, keeping well down till I got to a gap. It was dim and cool in the wood, and so lonely that I'd have been frightened if I hadn't a pocketful of paper and matches to keep me company. Bushes were covered in blackberries, and I stopped now and again to takc my pick, careful not to scratch myself or eat too many in case I got the gut ache when I went to bed at night.

It was long and narrow, not the sort of wood you could go deep into, so I jumped over a stream and found the middle quick enough, a clearing, more or less, with a dry and dying bush on one side that looked just ready for a fire. I worked like a galley slave, piling up dead twigs and leaves over my bit of paper that soon you could hardly see. I wondered about the noise but what could I do? and anyway soon forgot my worry and went on working. I knew it must be past dinner-time when I stood back to look at my bon-fire heap. Sweating like a bull (though nothing to how them trees would be sweating in a bit, I grinned) I measured the chances of a fire-engine fire: the bush was sure to light and so would the two small trees on either side but unless there was a good wind the main trees would be hard put to it.

The first match was slammed out by the wind that blew strong over my shoulder as if it had been lurking there specially; the head of the second fell off before I could get under the paper; the third-time lucky one caught a treat, was like a red, red robin breaking out of its shell, and I soon had to stand back to keep the burning blazes off my hand. I wanted to put it out at first: the words nearly choked me: "Stread on it. Kick it to bits." I twisted my hands up in front of me, but couldn't move, just stood there like the no good tripehound dad often called me (and which I dare say I was) until the smoke made me step further back—and back I went, until my head scraped into a big-barked tree. The noise of the fire must have been what frightened me: it was as hungry as if it had got teeth, went chewing its way up into the air like a shark in Technicolor. A stone of blood settled over my heart, but smoke and flame hypnotised me, stood me there frozen and happy, rubbing my hands yet wanting to put it out, but not being able to any more than I could kill myself.

I didn't know fires could grow like that. My little ones had always gone out, shrunk up to black bits and flew into the air when I set half a breath against it. But then, that was only true with a scrap of newspaper on an asphalt yard. This was in a wood, and fire took to it like a kid to hot dinners: it was a sheet of red flame and grey smoke, a choking wall and curtain that scared me a bit, because I was back to life, as if big hands would reach out and grab me in for good and all. Like my uncle had said hell was—though I never believed him till now.

It was time to run. I sped off like a rabbit, scratched and cindered as my ankles caught on thorns and sharp grass. The hammer-and-tongs of a fire-engine were a long way from me now, and I was a ragged-arsed thunderbolt suddenly tangled in a high bush, stuck like a press-stud that fought a path out, and went on again lit-up and cursing. At the edge of the wood I slowed down, and half-way to the lane looked back, expecting to see a sheet of fire and smoke bending out over the trees with flags flying and claws sharp.

But nothing. I could have burst into a gallon of tears. Nothing: not a butterfly of smoke, not an ant of flame. Maybe I'm too close to see, I thought. Or should I run back and stoke up again, blow it and coax, pat and kick it into life? But I went on. If the wood caught fire, as I still hoped, who'd get the fire-engines? And if nobody did would I hear and see them? Being as how I'd caused the fire I had to get miles away quick without being spotted, so how could I poke my nose in at the nearest copperbox and bawl out there was a fire in Snakey Wood and not risk getting sent to an approved school for my good deed? I wished I'd thought of this already, but all I could hope for now was that some bloke at the local sawmill or a field-digger from the farm would twig things while I wasn't too far off and get the fire-engine on its way so's I could run and see it.

By the lane I turned, and there it was: no fire yet but a thin trail of smoke coming up like a wavy blue pole above the crowded trees. I'd expected it all to be like it was on the pictures, boiling away and me having to run for my life, with a yellow-orange carpet of flame snap-dragging at my heels, but it just showed how different things were to what you expected. Not that I didn't know they always were, but it still came as a shock I don't mind admitting. The wood was burning, which was a start, and though I couldn't see any flame yet I didn't wait for it either, but dodged under the hedgebottom and crossed the open field to the big outstanding arm-beam of a canal lock. I puffed and grunted to get it shut, then crept across on all fours—using it as a bridge—to the towing path on the other side. Nobody saw me: a man was humped over the bank fishing a bit further down, but he never even turned to see who was passing. Maybe he ain't got a licence to fish, I thought, and no more wants to be seen than I do—which I can easy understand.

The wind blew stronger and the sun still shone but I daren't look back towards my pet wood which I hoped by now was crackling away to boggery. Walking along I looked like a fed-up kid out for an airing who was too daft and useless to have been in mischief—but because it seemed as if butter wouldn't melt in my mouth didn't mean I hadn't set a fire off in which butter wouldn't stand an earthly. I didn't want anybody to twig anything though, as I walked up to the main road and into a world of people and traffic where I wasn't so noticeable any more.

Back along the canal, far-off thick smoke was going up to the bubble-blue sky, black low down as if from an oil-well, but thinning a bit on top. It was burning all right, though people walking by didn't seem to think much was amiss. I sat on the bridge wall, unable to take my eyes off it, rattled a bit that people didn't turn to open their mouths and wonder what I was looking at. I wanted to shout out: "Hey missis, hey mester, see that smoke? It's Snakey Wood on fire, and I done it"—but somehow the words wouldn't come, though God knows I remember wanting them to.

I started off towards home, one minute happy that I'd brought off my own big fire, and the next crippled by a rotten sadness I couldn't explain, hands in pockets as I walked further and further away from the column of my fire and smoke that, if you think about it, should have made me the happiest kid in Radford.

From this changeable mood I was neither one thing nor the other as I went downhill towards the White Horse—almost home—having nothing else in my head but a shrill-whistled Al Jolson tune. Then into my ears and brain—through the last barbed-wire of my whistling—came the magic sound I'd longed all day to hear. The air went blue and electric, as it sometimes does before a terrible sheet-ripping thunderstorm, and cars at the crossroads stopped and waited, drivers winding their windows down to look out. My mouth opened and I stared and stared, the only picture in my mind for the next few seconds being that of the last bonfire night but one, in which I'd wandered off on my own up Mitchell Street and come across the best fire I'd ever seen. It was already twice as high as any man, and impossible to stoke anything else on top. A pile of mattresses still had got to be burned and a couple of big lads dragged them one at a time up on top of a chapel roof by whose side-walls the fire had been lit. When all of the two dozen bug-eaten mattresses were stacked high on the slates, the lads swung each one out, perched up there like demons in the blaze of the rattling flames, and let them crash down one by one into the very middle of the red bed. Everbody said the church would go, but it didn't, and when I saw that it wouldn't I walked away.

My eyes were open again on broad daylight, and from the top of the opposite hill sounded the bells I remembered hearing that very first time as a kid when downtown with mam. But this time there were more bells than I'd ever heard; a big red engine, fresh out of the vast sheds of town and coming between the shops and pubs, shot the cross-roads as if out of a flashgun, all bells at full throttle so that two blokes talking outside the pub couldn't make themselves heard and stopped till it had gone by. But they still couldn't start talking again, because another engine was almost right behind.

My legs trembled and I thought my ears would fall away from my head. One of the two men looked so hard at me that his face swam, and I thought: What's he making himself go all blurred like that for?—but when my ankles became heavy as lead and my legs above them turned into feathers I knew it was my eyes swimming, that I was about to cave in again like I'd done that long time ago with mam. I took a step forward, screwing my eyes and opening them, then held on the window ledge for a second, until I knew I'd be all right, and was able to stand another engine bursting in and out of my brain; then another.

Four! No sooner could I have shouted with joy, than I found it hard to stop myself letting the tears roll like wagons out of my eyes. I'd never seen four fire-engines before. The whole wood must be in flame from top to bottom, I thought, and was sorry now I hadn't stayed close by to watch, wondering if I should go back, because I knew that even four engines wouldn't get a fire like that down before tonight or even later. All that work and walking gone for nothing, I cursed, as another engine broke the record of the last one down the hill. I waved as it shot by yet felt as if I'd had my fill of fire-engines for a long while.

Six passed altogether. By this time I was sobbing, almost stone-dead and useless. "What's up, kid?" one of the two men said to me.

"I'm frightened," I managed to blurt out. He patted me on the shoulder. "There's no need o'that. The fire's miles away, up Wollaton somewhere, by the look on it. It wain't come down 'ere, so you needn't worry." But I couldn't stop. It was as hard to dry up as it had been for me to start, and I went on heaving as if the end of the world was just around the corner.

"Do you live far?" he asked.

"I'm frightened," was all I said, and he didn't know what to do, wished by this time he'd left me alone: "Well, you shouldn't be frightened. You're a big lad now."

I walked towards home along Eddison Road, my eyes drying up with every step, the great stone in my chest not jumping about so much. Six fire-engines made it a bigger day than Christmas, each red engine being better than a Santa Claus, so that even after my firebugging I never got over red being my favourite colour. When I went in through the scullery dad looked happy, and such a thing was hard for me to understand.

"Come on my old lad," he said. I'd never seen him so good-tempered. "Where've you bin all this time, you young bogger? It's nearly tea time." He pulled a chair to the table for me: "Here you are, get this down you. You must be clambed to death"—took a plate of dinner out of the oven. "I thought you'd got lost, or summat. Your mam's bin asking for you."

"Is she all right then, dad?"

"She's a bit better today," he smiled. "I expect we'll pull her through yet"—which I was so glad to hear that it made me twice as hungry, as if the fire had burned a hole in me as well as Snakey Wood, because a whole load of food was needed to fill it. Dad brought in the teapot, and I drank two mugs of that as well. "My Christ," he said, sitting opposite me with a fag on and enjoying the sight of me eating,

"I heard a lot of fire-engines going by just now. Some poor bogger's getting burned out of house and home by the sound of it."

Nobody knew who started that big fire all them years ago, and I know now that nobody will ever care, because Snakey Wood had gone forever, even better flattened than by any fire. Its trees have been ripped up and soil pressed down by a housing estate that spread over it. As it turned out I only burned down half, according to the *Post*, and though everybody in our yard knew I was a bit of a fire-bug nobody thought for a minute it might have been me who set fire to Snakey Wood. Or if they did, nowt was said.

In the next load of weeks and months I lost all interest in lighting fires. Even the sound of a fire-engine rattling by didn't bother me as much as it had. Maybe it was strange, me giving it up all of a sudden like that, but I just hadn't got the heart to put match to paper, couldn't be bothered in fact, after mam got better—which happened about the same time. I expect that big fire satisfied me, because whatever I did again would need to be bloody huge to get more than six engines called out to it. In any case there was something bigger than me to start fires, for after a couple of years came an air raid from the Germans and I remember getting out of the shelter at six one morning when the all clear had gone and standing in the middle of our street, seeing the whole sky red and orange over the other side of Nottingham—where, I heard later, two whole factories were up in flames. They burned for days, and I wanted to go off and see them but dad wouldn't let me. People said that fifty fire-engines had to come before that was put out—spinning into Nottingham from Mansfield and Derby and all over everywhere.

And not long afterwards I was fourteen, went to work and started courting, so what was the use of fires after that?

On Saturday Afternoon

I once saw a bloke try to kill himself. I'll never forget the day because I was sitting in the house one Saturday afternoon, feeling black and fed-up because everybody in the family had gone to the pictures, except me who'd for some reason been left out of it. 'Course, I didn't know then that I would soon see something you can never see in the same way on the pictures, a real bloke stringing himself up. I was only a kid at the time, so you can imagine how much I enjoyed it.

I've never known a family to look as black as our family when they're fed-up. I've seen the old man with his face so dark and full of murder because he ain't got no fags or was having to use saccharine to sweeten his tea, or even for nothing at all, that I've backed out of the house in case he got up from his fireside chair and came for me. He just sits, almost on top of the fire, his oil-stained Sunday-joint maulers opened out in front of him and facing inwards to each other, his thick shoulders scrunched forward, and his dark brown eyes staring into the fire. Now and again he'd say a dirty word, for no reason at all, the worst word you can think of, and when he starts saying this you know it's time to clear out. If mam's in it gets worse than ever, because she says sharp to him: "What are yo' looking so bleddy black for?" as if it might be because of something she's done, and before you know what's happening he's tipped up a tableful of pots and mam's gone out of the house crying. Dad hunches back over the fire and goes on swearing. All because of a packet of fags.

I once saw him broodier than I'd ever seen him, so that I thought he'd gone crackers in a quiet sort of way—until a fly flew to within a yard of him. Then his hand shot out, got it, and slung it crippled into the roaring fire. After that he cheered up a bit and mashed some tea.

Well, that's where the rest of us get our black looks from. It stands to reason we'd have them with a dad who carries on like that, don't it? Black looks run in the family. Some families have them and some don't. Our family has them right enough, and that's certain, so when we're fed-up we're really fed-up. Nobody knows why we get as fed-up as we do or why it gives us these black looks when we are. Some people get fed-up and don't look bad at all: they seem happy in a funny sort of way, as if they've just been set free from clink after being in there for something they didn't do, or come out of the pictures after sitting plugged for eight hours at a bad film, or just missed a bus they ran half a mile for and seen it was the wrong one just after they'd stopped running—but in our family it's murder for the others if one of us is fed-up. I've asked myself lots of times what it is, but I can never get any sort of answer even if I sit and think for hours, which I must admit I don't do, though it looks good when I say I do. But I sit and think for long enough, until mam says to me, at seeing me scrunched up over the fire like dad: "What are yo' looking so black for?" So I've just got to stop thinking about it in case I get really black and fed-up and go the same way as dad, tipping up a tableful of pots and all.

Mostly I suppose there's nothing to look so black for: though it's nobody's fault and you can't blame anyone for looking black because I'm sure it's summat in the blood. But on this Saturday afternoon I was looking so black that when dad came in from the bookie's he said to me: "What's up wi' yo'?"

"I feel badly," I fibbed. He'd have had a fit if I'd said I was only black because I hadn't gone to the pictures.

"Well have a wash," he told me.

"I don't want a wash," I said, and that was a fact.

"Well, get outside and get some fresh air then," he shouted.

I did as I was told, double-quick, because if ever dad goes as far as to tell me to get some fresh air I know it's time to get away from him. But outside the air wasn't so fresh, what with that bloody great bike factory bashing away at the yard-end. I didn't know where to go, so I walked up the yard a bit and sat down near somebody's back gate.

Then I saw this bloke who hadn't lived long in our yard. He was tall and thin and had a face like a parson except that he wore a flat cap and had a moustache that drooped, and looked as though he hadn't had a square meal for a year. I didn't think much o' this at the time: but I remember that as he turned in by the yard-end one of the nosy gossiping women who stood there every minute of the day except when she trudged to the pawnshop with her husband's bike or best suit, shouted to him: "What's that rope for, mate?"

He called back: "It's to 'ang messen wi', missis," and she crackled at this bloody good joke so loud and long you'd think she never heard such a good 'un, though the next day she crackled on the other side of her fat face.

He walked by me puffing a fag and carrying his coil of brand-new rope, and he had to step over me to get past. His boot nearly took my shoulder off, and when I told him to watch where he was going I don't think he heard me because he didn't even look round. Hardly anybody was about. All the kids were still at the pictures, and most of their mams and dads were downtown doing the shopping.

The bloke walked down the yard to his back door, and having nothing better to do because I hadn't gone to the pictures I followed him. You see, he left his back door open a bit, so I gave it a push and went in. I stood there, just watching him, sucking my thumb, the other hand in my pocket. I suppose he knew I was there, because his eyes were moving more natural now, but he didn't seem to mind. "What are yer going to do wi' that rope, mate?" I asked him.

"I'm going ter 'ang messen, lad," he told me, as though he'd done it a time or two already, and people had usually asked him questions like this beforehand.

"What for, mate?" He must have thought I was a nosy young bogger.

"Cause I want to, that's what for," he said, clearing

all the pots off the table and pulling it to the middle of the room. Then he stood on it to fasten the rope to the light-fitting. The table creaked and didn't look very safe, but it did him for what he wanted.

"It wain't hold up, mate," I said to him, thinking how much better it was being here than sitting in the pictures and seeing the Jungle Jim serial.

But he got nettled now and turned on me. "Mind yer own business."

I thought he was going to tell me to scram, but he didn't. He made ever such a fancy knot with that rope, as though he'd been a sailor or summat, and as he tied it he was whistling a fancy tune to himself. Then he got down from the table and pushed it back to the wall, and put a chair in its place. He wasn't looking black at all, nowhere near as black as anybody in our family when they're feeling fed-up. If ever he'd looked only half as black as our dad looked twice a week he'd have hanged himself years ago, I couldn't help thinking. But he was making a good job of that rope all right, as though he'd thought about it a lot anyway, and as though it was going to be the last thing he'd ever do. But I knew something he didn't know, because he wasn't standing where I was. I knew the rope wouldn't hold up, and I told him so, again.

"Shut yer gob," he said, but quiet like, "or I'll kick yer out."

I didn't want to miss it, so I said nothing. He took his cap off and put it on the dresser, then he took his coat off, and his scarf, and spread them out on the sofa. I wasn't a bit frightened, like I might be now at sixteen, because it was interesting. And being only ten I'd never had a chance to see a bloke hang himself before. We got pally, the two of us, before he slipped the rope around his neck.

"Shut the door," he asked me, and I did as I was told. "Ye're a good lad for your age," he said to me while I sucked my thumb, and he felt in his pockets and pulled out all that was inside, throwing the handful of bits and bobs on the table: fag-packet and peppermints, a pawn-ticket, an old comb, and a few coppers. He picked out a penny and gave it to me, saying: "Now listen ter me, young 'un. I'm going to 'ang messen, and when I'm swinging I want you to gi' this chair a bloody good kick and push it away. All right?"

I nodded.

He put the rope around his neck, and then took it off like it was a tie that didn't fit. "What are yer going to do it for, mate?" I asked again.

"Because I'm fed-up," he said, looking very unhappy. "And because I want to. My missus left me, and I'm out o' work."

I didn't want to argue, because the way he said it, I knew he couldn't do anything else except hang himself. Also there was a funny look in his face: even when he talked to me I swear he couldn't see me. It was different to the black looks my old man puts on, and I suppose that's why my old man would never hang himself, worse luck, because he never gets a look into his clock like this bloke had. My old man's look stares *at* you, so that you have to back down and fly out of the house: this bloke's look looked *through* you, so that you could face it and know it wouldn't do you any harm. So I saw now that dad would never hang himself because he could never get the right sort of look into his face, in spite of the fact that he'd been out of work often enough. Maybe mam would have to leave him first, and then he might do it; but no—I shook my head—there wasn't much chance of that even though he did lead her a dog's life.

"Yer wain't forget to kick that chair away?" he reminded me, and I swung my head to say I wouldn't. So my eyes were popping and I watched every move he made. He stood on the chair and put the rope around his neck so that it fitted this time, still whistling his fancy tune. I wanted to get a better goz at the knot, because my pal was in the Scouts, and would ask to know how it was done, and if I told him later he'd let me know what happened at the pictures in the Jungle Jim serial, so's I could have my cake and eat it as well, as mam says, tit for tat. But I thought I'd better not ask the bloke to tell me, and I stayed back in my corner.

The last thing he did was take the wet dirty butt-end from his lips and sling it into the empty firegrate, following it with his eyes to the black fireback where it landed—as if he was then going to mend a fault in the lighting like any electrician.

Suddenly his long legs wriggled and his feet tried to kick the chair, so I helped him as I'd promised I would and took a runner at it as if I was playing centre-forward for Notts Forest, and the chair went scooting back against the sofa, dragging his muffler to the floor as it tipped over. He swung for a bit, his arms chafing like he was a scarecrow flapping birds away, and he made a noise in his throat as if he'd just took a dose of salts and was trying to make them stay down.

Then there was another sound, and I looked up and saw a big crack come in the ceiling, like you see on the pictures when an earthquake's happening, and the bulb began circling round and round as though it was a space ship. I was just beginning to get dizzy when, thank Christ, he fell down with such a horrible thump on the floor that I thought he'd broke every bone he'd got. He kicked around for a bit, like a dog that's got colic bad. Then he lay still.

I didn't stay to look at him. "I told him that rope wouldn't hold up," I kept saying to myself as I went out of the house, tut-tutting because he hadn't done the job right, hands stuffed deep into my pockets and nearly crying at the balls-up he'd made of everything. I slammed his gate so hard with disappointment that it nearly dropped off its hinges.

Just as I was going back up the yard to get my tea at home, hoping the others had come back from the pictures so's I wouldn't have anything to keep on being black about, a copper passed me and headed for the bloke's door. He was striding quickly with his head bent forward, and I knew that somebody had narked. They must have seen him buy the rope and then tipped-off the cop. Or happen the old hen at the yard-end had finally caught on. Or perhaps he'd even told somebody himself, because I supposed that the bloke who'd strung himself up hadn't much known what he was doing, especially with the look I'd seen in his eyes. But that's how it is, I said to myself, as I followed the copper back to the bloke's house, a poor bloke can't even hang himself these days.

When I got back the copper was slitting the rope from his neck with a pen-knife, then he gave him a drink of water, and the bloke opened his peepers. I didn't like the copper, because he'd got a couple of my mates sent to approved school for pinching lead piping from lavatories.

"What did you want to hang yourself for?" he asked the bloke, trying to make him sit up. He could hardly talk, and one of his hands was bleeding from where the light-bulb had smashed. I knew that rope wouldn't hold up, but he hadn't listened to me. I'll never hang myself anyway, but if I want to I'll make sure I do it from a tree or something like that, not a light fitting. "Well, what did you do it for?"

"Because I wanted to," the bloke croaked.

"You'll get five years for this," the copper told him. I'd crept back into the house and was sucking my thumb in the same corner.

"That's what yo' think," the bloke said, a normal frightened look in his eyes now. "I only wanted to hang myself."

"Well," the copper said, taking out his book, "it's against the law, you know."

"Nay," the bloke said, "it can't be. It's my life, ain't it?"

"You might think so," the copper said, "but it ain't."

He began to suck the blood from his hand. It was such a little scratch though that you couldn't see it. "That's the first thing I knew," he said.

"Well I'm telling you," the copper told him.

'Course, I didn't let on to the copper that I'd helped the bloke to hang himself. I wasn't born yesterday, nor the day before yesterday either.

"It's a fine thing if a bloke can't tek his own life", the bloke said, seeing he was in for it.

"Well he can't," the copper said, as if reading out of his book and enjoying it. "It ain't your life. And it's a crime to take your own life. It's killing yourself. It's suicide."

The bloke looked hard, as if every one of the copper's words meant six-months cold. I felt sorry for him, and that's a fact, but if only he'd listened to what I'd said and not depended on that light-fitting. He should have done it from a tree, or something like that.

He went up the yard with the copper like a peaceful lamb, and we all thought that that was the end of that.

But a couple of days later the news was flashed through to us—even before it got to the *Post* because a woman in our yard worked at the hospital of an evening dishing grub out and tidying up. I heard her spilling it to somebody at the yard-end. "I'd never 'ave thought it. I thought he'd got that daft idea out of his head when they took him away. But no. Wonders'll never cease. Chucked 'issen from the hospital window when the copper who sat near his bed went off for a pee. Would you believe it? Dead? Not much 'e ain't."

He'd heaved himself at the glass, and fallen like a stone on to the road. In one way I was sorry he'd done it, but in another I was glad, because he'd proved to the coppers and everybody whether it was his life or not all right. It was marvellous though, the way the brainless bastards had put him in a ward six floors up, which finished him off, proper, even better than a tree.

All of which will make me think twice about how black I sometimes feel. The black coal-bag locked inside you, and the black look it puts on your face, doesn't mean you're going to string yourself up or sling yourself under a double-decker or chuck yourself out of a window or cut your throat with a sardine-tin or put your head in the gas-oven or drop your rotten sack-bag of a body on to a railway line, because when you're feeling that black you can't even move from your chair. Anyhow, I know I'll never get so black as to hang myself, because hanging don't look very nice to me, and never will, the more I remember old what's-his-name swinging from the light-fitting.

More than anything else, I'm glad now I didn't go to the pictures that Saturday afternoon when I was feeling black and ready to do myself in. Because you know, I shan't ever kill myself. Trust me. I'll stay alive half-barmy till I'm a hundred and five, and then go out screaming blue murder because I want to stay where I am.

Uncle Ernest

A middle-aged man wearing a dirty raincoat, who badly needed a shave and looked as though he hadn't washed for a month, came out of a public lavatory with a cloth bag of tools folded beneath his arm. Standing for a moment on the edge of the pavement to adjust his cap—the cleanest thing about him—he looked casually to left and right and, when the flow of traffic had eased off, crossed the road. His name and trade were always spoken in one breath, even when the nature of his trade was not in question: Ernest Brown the upholsterer. Every night before returning to his lodgings he left the bag of tools for safety with a man who looked after the public lavatory near the town centre, for he felt there was a risk of them being lost or stolen should he take them back to his room, and if such a thing were to happen his living would be gone.

Chimes to the value of half-past ten boomed from the Council-house clock. Over the theatre patches of blue sky held hard-won positions against autumnal clouds, and a treacherous wind lashed out its gusts, sending paper and cigarette packets cartwheeling along unswept gutters. Empty-bellied Ernest was ready for his breakfast, so walked through a café doorway, instinctively lowering his head as he did so, though the beams were a foot above his height.

The long spacious eating-place was almost full. Ernest usually arrived for his breakfast at nine o'clock but having been paid ten pounds for re-covering a three-piece in a public house the day before, he had stationed himself in the Saloon Bar for the rest of the evening to drink jar after jar of beer, in a slow prolonged and concentrated way that lonely men have. As a result it had been difficult to drag himself from drugged and blissful sleep this morning. His face was pale and his eyes an unhealthy yellow: when he spoke only a few solitary teeth showed behind his lips.

Having passed through the half dozen noisy people standing about he found himself at the counter, a scarred and chipped haven for hands, like a littered invasion beach extending between two headlands of tea-urns. The big fleshy brunette was busy, so he hastily scanned the list written out in large white letters on the wall behind. He made a timid gesture with his hand. "A cup of tea, please."

The brunette turned on him. Tea swilled from a huge brown spout—into a cup that had a crack emerging like a hair above the layer of milk—and a spoon clinked after it into the steam. "Anything else?"

He spoke up hesitantly. "Tomatoes on toast as well." Picking up the plate pushed over to him he moved slowly backwards out of the crowd, then turned and walked towards a vacant corner table.

A steamy appetizing smell rose from the plate: he took up the knife and fork and, with the sharp clean action of a craftsman, cut off a corner of the toast and tomato and raised it slowly to his mouth, eating with relish and hardly noticing people sitting roundabout. Each wielding of his knife and fork, each geometrical cut of the slice of toast, each curve and twist of his lips joined in a complex and regular motion that gave him great satisfaction. He ate slowly, quietly and contentedly, aware only of himself and his body being warmed and made tolerable once more by food. The leisurely movement of spoon and cup and saucer made up the familiar noise of late breakfast in a crowded café sounded like music flowing here and there in variations of rhythm.

For years he had eaten alone, but was not yet accustomed to loneliness. He could not get used to it, had only adapted himself to it temporarily in the hope that one day its spell would break. Ernest remembered little of his past, and life moved under him so that he hardly noticed its progress. There was no strong memory to entice him to what had gone by, except that of dead and dying men, straggling barbed-wire between the trenches in the first world war. Two sentences had dominated his lips during the years that followed: "I should not be here in England. I should be dead with the rest of them in France." Time bereft him of these sentences, till only a dull wordless image remained.

People, he found, treated him as if he were a ghost, as if he were not made of flesh and blood—or so it seemed—and from then on he had lived alone. His wife left him—due to his too vile temper, it was said—and his brothers went to other towns. Later he had thought to look them up, but decided against it: for even in this isolation only the will to go forward and accept more of it seemed worth while. He felt in a dim indefinite way that to go back and search out the slums and landmarks of his youth, old friends, the smells and sounds that beckoned him tangibly from better days, was a sort of death. He argued that it was best to leave them alone, because it seemed somehow probable that after death—whenever it came—he would meet all these things once again.

No pink scar marked his flesh from shell-shock and a jolted brain, and so what had happened in the war warranted no pension book, and even to him the word "injury" never came into his mind. It was just that he did not care any more: the wheel of the years had broken him, and so had made life tolerable. When the next war came his back was not burdened at first, and even the fines and days in prison that he was made to pay for being without Identity Card or Ration Book—or for giving them away with a glad heart to deserters—did not lift him from his tolerable brokenness. The nightmare hours of gunfire and exploding bombs revived a dull image long suppressed as he stared blankly at the cellar wall of his boarding house, and even threw into his mind the scattered words of two insane sentences. But, considering the time-scale his life was lived on, the war ended quickly, and again nothing mattered. He lived from hand to mouth, working cleverly at settees and sofas and chairs, caring about no one. When work was difficult to find and life was hard, he did not notice it very much, and now that he was prosperous and had enough money, he also detected little difference, spending what he earned on beer, and never once thinking that he needed a new coat or solid pair of boots.

He lifted the last piece of toast and tomato from his plate, then felt dregs of tea moving against his teeth. When he had finished chewing he lit a cigarette and was once more aware of people sitting around him. It was eleven o'clock and the low-roofed café was slowly emptying, leaving only a dozen people inside. He knew that at one table they were talking about horse-racing and at another about war, but words only flowed into his ears and entered his mind at a low pitch of comprehension, leaving it calm and content as he vaguely contemplated the positions and patterns of tables about the room. There would be no work until two o'clock, so he intended sitting where he was until then. Yet a sudden embarrassment at having no food on the table to justify a prolonged occupation of it sent him to the counter for tea and cakes.

As he was being served two small girls came in. One sat at a table, but the second and elder stood at the counter. When he returned to his place he found the younger girl sitting there. He was confused and shy, but nevertheless sat down to drink tea and cut a cake into four pieces. The girl looked at him and continued to do so until the elder one came from the counter carrying two cups of steaming tea.

They sat talking and drinking, utterly oblivious of Ernest, who slowly felt their secretive, childish animation enter into himself. He glanced at them from time to time, feeling as if he should not be there, though when he looked at them he did so in a gentle way, with kind, full-smiling eyes. The elder girl, about twelve years old, was dressed in a brown coat that was too big for her, and though she was talking and laughing most of the time he noticed the paleness of her face and her large round eyes that he would have thought beautiful had he not detected the familiar type of vivacity that expressed neglect and want.

The smaller girl was less lively and merely smiled as she answered her sister with brief curt words. She drank her tea and warmed her hands at the same time without putting the cup down once until she had emptied it. Her thin red fingers curled around the cup as she stared into the leaves, and gradually the talk between them died down and they were silent, leaving the field free for traffic that could be heard moving along the street outside, and for inside noises made by the brunette who washed cups and dishes ready for the rush that was expected at midday dinner-time.

Ernest was calculating how many yards of rexine would be needed to cover the job he was to do that afternoon, but when the younger girl began speaking he listened to her, hardly aware that he was doing so.

"If you've got any money I'd like a cake, our Alma."

"I haven't got any more money," the elder one replied impatiently.

"Yes you have, and I'd like a cake."

She was adamant, almost aggressive. "Then you'll have to want on, because I've only got tuppence."

"You can buy a cake with that," the young girl persisted, twining her fingers around the empty cup. "We don't need bus fares home because it ain't far to walk."

"We can't walk home: it might rain."

"No it won't."

"Well I want a cake as well, but I'm not walking all that way," the elder girl said conclusively, blocking any last gap that might remain in her defences. The younger girl gave up and said nothing, looked emptily in front of her.

Ernest had finished eating and took out a cigarette, struck a match across the iron fastening of a table leg and, having inhaled deeply, allowed smoke to wander from his mouth. Like a gentle tide washing in under the moon, a line of water flowing inwards and covering the sand, a feeling of acute loneliness took hold of him, an agony that would not let him weep. The two girls sat before him wholly engrossed in themselves, still debating whether they should buy a cake, or whether they should ride home on a bus.

"But it'll be cold," reasoned the elder, "walking home."

"No it won't," the other said, but with no conviction in her words. The sound of their voices told him how lonely he was, each word feeding him with so much more loneliness that he felt utterly unhappy and empty.

Time went slowly: the minute-hand of the clock seemed as if it were nailed immovably at one angle. The two girls looked at each other and did not notice him: he withdrew into himself and felt the emptiness of the world and wondered how he would spend all the days that seemed to stretch vacantly, like goods on a broken-down conveyor belt, before him. He tried to remember things that had happened and felt panic when he discovered a thirty-year vacuum. All he could see behind was a grey mist and all he could see before him was the same unpredictable fog that would hide nothing. He wanted to walk out of the café and find some activity so that he would henceforth be able to mark off the passage of his empty days, but he had no will to move. He heard someone crying so shook himself free of such thoughts and saw the younger girl with hands to her eyes, weeping. "What's the matter?" he asked tenderly, leaning across the table.

The elder girl replied for her, saying sternly:

"Nothing. She's acting daft."

"But she must be crying for some reason. What is it?" Ernest persisted, quietly and soothingly, bending closer still towards her. "Tell me what's wrong." Then he remembered something. He drew it like a live thread from a mixture of reality and dream, hanging on to vague words that floated back into his mind. The girls' conversation came to him through an intricate process of recollection. "I'll get you something to eat," he ventured. "Can I?"

She unscrewed clenched fingers from her eyes and looked up, while the elder girl glared at him resentfully and said: "We don't want anything. We're going now."

"No, don't go," he cried. "You just sit down and see what I'm going to get for you." He stood up and walked to the counter, leaving them whispering to each other.

He came back with a plate of pastries and two cups of tea, which he set before the girls, who looked on in silence. The younger was smiling now. Her round eager eyes were fascinated, yet followed each movement of his hands with some apprehension. Though still hostile the elder girl was gradually subdued by the confidently working actions of his hands, by caressing words and the kindness that showed in his face. He was wholly absorbed in doing good and, at the same time, fighting the feeling of loneliness that he still remembered, but only as a nightmare is remembered.

The two children fell under his spell, began to eat cakes and sip the tea. They glanced at each other, and then at Ernest as he sat before them smoking a cigarette. The café was still almost empty, and the few people eating were so absorbed in themselves, or were in so much of a hurry to eat their food and get out that they took little notice of the small company in the corner. Now that the atmosphere between himself and the two girls had grown more friendly Ernest began to talk to them. "Do you go to school?" he asked.

The elder girl automatically assumed control and answered his questions. "Yes, but today we had to come down town on an errand for our mam."

"Does your mother go out to work, then?"

"Yes," she informed him. "All day."

Ernest was encouraged. "And does she cook your dinners?"

She obliged him with another answer. "Not until night."

"What about your father?" he went on.

"He's dead," said the smaller girl, her mouth filled with food, daring to speak outright for the first time. Her sister looked at her with disapproval, making it plain that she had said the wrong thing and that she should only speak under guidance.

"Are you going to school then this afternoon?" Ernest resumed.

"Yes," the spokesman said.

He smiled at her continued hard control. "And what's your name then?"

"Alma," she told him, "and hers is Joan." She indicated the smaller girl with a slight nod of the head.

"Are you often hungry?"

She stopped eating and glanced at him, uncertain how to

answer. "No, not much," she told him non-committally, busily eating a second pastry.

"But you were today?"

"Yes," she said, casting away diplomacy like the crumpled cake-paper she let fall to the floor.

He said nothing for a few moments, sitting with knuckles pressed to his lips. "Well, look"—he began suddenly talking again—"I come in here every day for my dinner, just about half-past twelve, and if ever you're feeling hungry, come down and see me."

They agreed to this, accepted sixpence for their bus fares home, thanked him very much, and said good-bye.

During the following weeks they came to see him almost every day. Sometimes, when he had little money, he filled his empty stomach with a cup of tea while Alma and Joan satisfied themselves on five shillings'-worth of more solid food. But he was happy and gained immense satisfaction from seeing them bending hungrily over eggs, bacon and pastries, and he was so smoothed at last into a fine feeling of having something to live for that he hardly remembered the lonely days when his only hope of being able to talk to someone was by going into a public house to get drunk. He was happy now because he had his 'little girls' to look after, as he came to call them.

He began spending all his money to buy them presents, so that he was often in debt at his lodgings. He still did not buy any clothes, for whereas in the past his money had been swilled away on beer, now it was spent on presents and food for the girls, and he went on wearing the same old dirty mackintosh and was still without a collar to his shirt; even his cap was no longer clean.

Every day, straight out of school, Alma and Joan ran to catch a bus for the town centre and, a few minutes later, smiling and out of breath, walked into the café where Ernest was waiting. As days and weeks passed, and as Alma noticed how much Ernest depended on them for company, how happy he was to see them, and how obviously miserable when they did not come for a day—which was rare now—she began to demand more and more presents, more food, more money, but only in a particular naïve and childish way, so that Ernest, in his oblivious contentment, did not notice it.

But certain customers of the café who came in every day could not help but see how the girls asked him to buy them this and that, and how he always gave in with a nature too good to be decently true, and without the least sign of realizing what was really happening. He would never dream to question their demands, for to him, these two girls whom he looked upon almost as his own daughters were the only people he had to love.

Ernest, about to begin eating, noticed two smartly dressed men sitting at a table a few yards away. They had sat in the same place the previous day, and also the day before that, but he thought no more about it because Joan and Alma came in and walked quickly across to his table.

"Hello Uncle Ernest!" they said brightly. "What can we have for dinner?" Alma looked across at the chalk-written list on the wall to read what dishes were available.

His face changed from the blank preoccupation of eating, and a smile of happiness infused his cheeks, eyes, and the curve of his lips. "Whatever you like," he answered.

"But what have they got?" Alma demanded crossly. "I can't read their scrawl."

"Go up to the counter and ask for a dinner," he advised with a laugh.

"Will you give me some money then?" she asked her hand out. Joan stood by without speaking, lacking Alma's confidence, her face timid, and nervous because she did not yet understand this regular transaction of money between Ernest and themselves, being afraid that one day they would stand there waiting for money and Ernest would quite naturally look surprised and say there was nothing for them.

He had just finished repairing an antique three-piece and had been paid that morning, so Alma took five shillings and they went to the counter for a meal. While they were waiting to be served the two well-dressed men who had been watching Ernest for the last few days stood up and walked over to him.

Only one of them spoke; the other held his silence and looked on, "Are those two girls your daughters, or any relation to you?" the first asked, nodding towards the counter.

Ernest looked up and smiled. "No," he explained in a mild voice "they'r just friends of mine, why?"

The man's eyes were hard, and he spoke clearly, "What kind of friends?"

"Just friends. Why? Who are you?" He shuddered, feeling a kind of half-guilt growing inside him for a half-imagined reason that he hoped wasn't true.

"Never mind who we are. I just want you to answer my question."

Ernest raised his voice slightly, yet did not dare to look into the man's arrogant eyes. "Why?" he cried. "What's it got to do with you? Why are you asking questions like this?"

"We're from the police station," the man remarked dryly, "and we've had complaints that you'ar giving these little girls money and leading them the wrong way!"

Ernest wanted to laugh, but only from misery. Yet he did not want to laugh in case he should annoy the two detectives. He started to talk: "But . . . but . . ." then found himself unable to go on. There was much that he wanted to say, yet he could enunciate nothing, and a bewildered animal stare moved slowly into his eyes.

"Look," the man said emphatically, "we don't want any of your 'buts'. We know all about you. We know who you are. We've known you for years in fact, and we're asking you to leave those girls alone and have nothing more to do with them. Men like you shouldn't give money to little girls. You should know what you're doing, and have more sense."

Ernest protested loudly at last. "I tell you they're friends of mine. I mean no harm I look after them and give them presents just as I would daughters of my own. They're the only company I've got. In any case why shouldn't I look after them? Why should you take them away from me? Who do you think you are? Leave me alone . . . leave me alone." His voice had risen to a weak scream of defiance, and the other people in the crowded café were looking around and staring at him, wondering what was the cause of the disturbance.

The two detectives acted quickly and competently, yet without apparent haste. One stood on each side of him, lifted him up, and walked him by the counter, out on to the street, squeezing his wrists tightly as they did so. As Ernest passed the counter he saw the girls holding their plates, looking in fear and wonder at him being walked out.

They took him to the end of the street, and stood there for a few seconds talking to him, still keeping hold of his wrists and pressing their fingers hard into them.

"Now look here, we don't want any more trouble from *you*, but if ever we see you near those girls again, you'll find yourself up before a magistrate." The tone of finality in his voice possessed a physical force that pushed Ernest to the brink of sanity.

He stood speechless. He wanted to say so many things, but the words would not come to his lips. They quivered helplessly with shame and hatred, and so were incapable of making words. "We're asking you in a peaceful manner," the detective went on, "to leave them alone. Understand?"

"Yes," Ernest was forced to answer.

"Right. Go on then. And we don't want to see you with those girls again."

He was only aware of the earth sliding away from under his feet, and a wave of panic crashing into his mind, and he felt the unbearable and familiar emptiness that flowed outwards from a tiny and unknowable point inside him. Then he was filled with hatred for everything, then intense pity for all the movement that was going on around him, and finally even more intense pity for himself. He wanted to cry but could not: he could only walk away from his shame.

Then he began to shed agony at each step. His bitterness eddied away and a feeling the depth of which he had never known before took its place. There was now more purpose in the motion of his footsteps as he went along the pavement through midday crowds. And it seemed to him that he did not care about anything any more as he pushed through the swing doors and walked into the crowded and noisy bar of a public house, his stare fixed by a beautiful heavily baited trap of beer pots that would take him into the one and only best kind of oblivion.

The Fishing-boat Picture

I've been a postman for twenty-eight years. Take that first sentence: because it's written in a simple way may make the fact of my having been a postman for so long seem important, but I realise that such a fact has no significance whatever. After all, it's not my fault that it may seem as if it has to some people just because I wrote it down plain; I wouldn't know how to do it any other way. If I started using long and complicated words that I'd searched for in the dictionary I'd use them too many times, the same ones over and over again, with only a few sentences—if that—between each one; so I'd rather not make what I'm going to write look foolish by using dictionary words.

It's also twenty-eight years since I got married. That statement is very important no matter how you write it or in what way you look at it. It so happened that I married my wife as soon as I got a permanent job, and the first good one I landed was with the Post Office (before that I'd been errand-boy and mash-lad). I had to marry her as soon as I got a job because I'd promised her I would, and she wasn't the sort of person to let me forget it.

When my first pay night came I called for her and asked: "What about a walk up Snakey Wood?" I was cheeky-daft and on top of the world, and because I'd forgotten about our arrangement I didn't think it strange at all when she said: "Yes, all right." It was late autumn I remember and the leaves were as high as snow, crisp on top but soggy underneath. In the full moon and light wind we walked over the Cherry Orchard, happy and arm-in-arm. Suddenly she stopped and turned to me, a big-boned girl yet with a good figure and a nice enough face: "Do you want to go into the wood?"

What a thing to ask! I laughed: "You know I do. Don't you?"

We walked on, and a minute later she said: "Yes, I do; but you know what we're to do now you've got a steady job, don't you?"

I wondered what it was all about. Yet I knew right enough. "Get married," I admitted, adding on second thoughts: "I don't have much of a wage to be wed on, you know."

"It's enough, as far as I'm concerned," she answered.

And that was that. She gave me the best kiss I'd ever had, and then we went into the wood.

She was never happy about our life together, right from the start. And neither was I, because it didn't take her long to begin telling me that all her friends—her family most of all—said time and time again that our marriage wouldn't last five minutes. I could never say much back to this, knowing after the first few months how right everybody would be. Not that it bothered me though, because I was always the sort of bloke that doesn't get ruffled at anything. If you want to know the truth—the sort of thing I don't suppose many blokes would he ready to admit—the bare fact of my getting married meant only that I changed one house and one mother for another house and a different mother. It was as simple as that. Even my wage-packet didn't alter its course: I handed it over every Friday night and got five shillings back for tobacco and a visit to the pictures. It was the sort of wedding where the cost of the ceremony and reception go as a down payment, and you then continue dishing-out your wages every week for life. Which is where I suppose they got this hire purchase idea from.

But our marriage lasted for more than the five minutes everybody prophesied: it went on for six years; she left me when I was thirty, and when she was thirty-four. The trouble was that when we had a row—and they were rows, swearing, hurling pots: the lot—it was too much like suffering, and in the middle of them it seemed to me as if we'd done nothing but row and suffer like this from the moment we set eyes on each other, with not a moment's break, and that it would go on like this for as long as we stayed together. The truth was, as I see it now—and even saw it sometimes then—that a lot of our time was bloody enjoyable.

I'd had an idea before she went that our time as man and wife was about up, because one day we had the worst fight of them all. We were sitting at home one evening after tea, one at each end of the table, plates empty and bellies full so that there was no excuse for what followed. My head was in a book, and Kathy just sat there.

Suddenly she said: "I do love you, Harry." I didn't hear the words for some time, as is often the case when you're reading a book. Then: "Harry, look at me."

My face came up, smiled, and went down again to my reading. Maybe I was in the wrong, and should have said something, but the book was too good.

"I'm sure all that reading's bad for your eyes," she commented, prising me again from the hot possessive world of India.

"It ain't," I denied, not looking up. She was young and still fair-faced, a passionate loose-limbed thirty-odd that wouldn't let me sidestep either her obstinacy or anger. "My dad used to say that on'y fools read books, because, they'd such a lot to learn."

The words hit me and sank in, so that I couldn't resist coming back with, still not looking up: "He on'y said that because he didn't know how to read. He was jealous, if you ask me."

"No need to be jealous of the rammel you stuff your big head with," she said, slowly to make sure I knew she meant every word. The print wouldn't stick any more; the storm was too close.

"Look, why don't *you* get a book, duck?" But she never would, hated them like poison.

She sneered: "I've got more sense; and too much to do."

Then I blew up, in a mild way because I still hoped she wouldn't take on, that I'd be able to finish my chapter. "Well let me read, anyway, wain't you? It's an interesting book, and I'm tired."

But such a plea only gave her another opening. "Tired?

You're allus tired." She laughed out loud: "Tired Tim! You ought to do some real work for a change instead of walking the streets with that daft post bag."

I won't go on, spinning it out word for word. In any case not many more passed before she snatched the book out of my hands. "You booky bastard," she screamed, "nowt but books, books, books, you bleddy dead-'ead"—and threw the book on the heaped-up coals, working it further and further into their blazing middle with the poker.

This annoyed me, so I clocked her one, not very hard, but I did. It was a good reading-book, and what's more it belonged to the library. I'd have to pay for a new one. She slammed out of the house, and I didn't see her until next day.

I didn't think to break my heart very much when she skipped off. I'd had enough. All I can say is that it was a stroke of God's luck we never had any kids. She was confined once or twice, but it never came to anything; each time it dragged more bitterness out of her than we could absorb in the few peaceful months that came between. It might have been better if she'd had kids though; you never know.

A month after burning the book she ran off with a housepainter. It was all done very nicely. There was no shouting or knocking each other about or breaking up the happy home. I just came back from work one day and found a note waiting for me. "I am going away and not coming back"—propped on the mantelpiece in front of the clock. No tear stains on the paper, just eight words in pencil on a page of the insurance book—I've still got it in the back of my wallet, though God knows why.

The housepainter she went with had lived in a house on his own, across the terrace. He'd been on the dole for a few months and suddenly got a job at a place twenty miles away I was later told. The neighbours seemed almost eager to let me know—after they'd gone, naturally—that they'd been knocking-on together for about a year. No one knew where they'd skipped off to exactly, probably imagining that I wanted to chase after them. But the idea never occurred to me. In any case what was I to do? Knock him flat and drag Kathy back by the hair? Not likely.

Even now it's no use trying to tell myself that I wasn't disturbed by this change in my life. You miss a woman when she's been living with you in the same house for six years, no matter what sort of cat-and-dog life you led together—though we had our moments, that I will say. After her sudden departure there was something different about the house, about the walls, ceiling and every object in it. And something altered inside me as well—though I tried to tell myself that all was just the same and that Kathy's leaving me wouldn't make a blind bit of difference. Nevertheless time crawled at first, and I felt like a man just learning to pull himself along with a clubfoot; but then the endless evenings of summer came and I was happy almost against my will, too happy anyway to hang on to such torments as sadness and loneliness. The world was moving and, I felt, so was I.

In other words I succeeded in making the best of things, which as much as anything else meant eating a good meal at the canteen every midday. I boiled an egg for breakfast (fried with bacon on Sundays) and had something cold but solid for my tea every night. As things went, it wasn't a bad life. It might have been a bit lonely, but at least it was peaceful, and it got as I didn't mind it, one way or the other. I even lost the feeling of loneliness that had set me thinking a bit too much just after she'd gone. And then I didn't dwell on it any more. I saw enough people on my rounds during the day to last me through the evenings and at week-ends. Sometimes I played draughts at the club, or went out for a slow half pint to the pub up the street.

Things went on like this for ten years. From what I gathered later Kathy had been living in Leicester with her house-painter. Then she came back to Nottingham. She came to see me one Friday evening, payday. From her point of view, as it turned out, she couldn't have come at a better time.

I was leaning on my gate in the backyard smoking a pipe of tobacco. I'd had a busy day on my rounds, an irritating time of it—being handed back letters all along the line, hearing that people had left and that no one had any idea where they'd moved to; and other people taking as much as ten minutes to get out of bed and sign for a registered letter—and now I felt twice as peaceful because I was at home, smoking my pipe in the backyard at the fag-end of an autumn day. The sky was a clear yellow, going green above the housetops and wireless aerials. Chimneys were just beginning to send out evening smoke, and most of the factory motors had been switched off. The noise of kids scooting around lamp-posts and the barking of dogs came from what sounded a long way off. I was about to knock my pipe out, to go back into the house and carry on reading a book about Brazil I'd left off the night before.

As soon as she came around the corner and started walking up the yard I knew her. It gave me a funny feeling, though: ten years ain't enough to change anybody so's you don't recognise them, but it's long enough to make you have to look twice before you're sure. And that split second in between is like a kick in the stomach. She didn't walk with her usual gait, as though she owned the terrace and everybody in it. She was a bit slower than when I'd seen her last, as if she'd bumped into a wall during the last ten years through walking in the cock o' the walk way she'd always had. She didn't seem so sure of herself and was fatter now, wearing a frock left over from the summer and an open winter coat, and her hair had been dyed fair whereas it used to be a nice shade of brown.

I was neither glad nor unhappy to see her, but maybe that's what shock does, because I was surprised, that I will say. Not that I never expected to see her again, but you know how it is, I'd just forgotten her somehow. The longer she was away our married life shrunk to a year, a month, a day, a split second of sparking light I'd met in the black darkness before getting up time. The memory had drawn itself too far back, even in ten years, to remain as anything much more than a dream. For as soon as I got used to living alone I forgot her.

Even though her walk had altered I still expected her to say something sarky like: "Didn't expect to see me back at the scene of the crime so soon, did you, Harry?" Or: "You thought it wasn't true that a bad penny always turns up again, didn't you?"

But she just stood. "Hello, Harry"—waited for me to lean up off the gate so's she could get in. "It's been a long time since we saw each other, hasn't it?"

I opened the gate, slipping my empty pipe away. "Hello, Kathy," I said, and walked down the yard so that she could come behind me. She buttoned her coat as we went into the kitchen, as though she were leaving the house instead of just going in. "How are you getting on then?" I asked, standing near the fireplace.

Her back was to the wireless, and it didn't seem as if she wanted to look at me. Maybe I was a bit upset after all at her sudden visit, and it's possible I showed it without knowing it at the time, because I filled my pipe up straightaway, a thing I never normally do. I always let one pipe cool down before lighting the next.

"I'm fine," was all she'd say.

"Why don't you sit down then, Kath? I'll get you a bit of a fire soon."

She kept her eyes to herself still, as if not daring to look at the old things around her, which were much as they'd been when she left. However she'd seen enough to remark: "You look after yourself all right."

"What did you expect?" I said, though not in a sarcastic way. She wore lipstick, I noticed, which I'd never seen on her before, and rouge, maybe powder as well, making her look old in a different way, I supposed, than if she'd had nothing on her face at all. It was a thin disguise, yet sufficient to mask from me—and maybe her—the person she'd been ten years ago.

"I hear there's a war coming on," she said, for the sake of talking.

I pulled a chair away from the table. "Come on, sit down, Kathy. Get that weight off your legs"—an old phrase we'd used though I don't know why I brought it out at that moment. "No, I wouldn't be a bit surprised. That bloke Hitler wants a bullet in his brain—like a good many Germans." I looked up and caught her staring at the picture of a fishing boat on the wall: brown and rusty with sails half spread in a bleak sunrise, not far from the beach along which a woman walked bearing a basket of fish on her shoulder. It was one of a set that Kathy's brother had given us as a wedding present, the other two having been smashed up in another argument we'd had. She liked it a lot, this remaining fishing-boat picture. The last of the fleet, we used to call it, in our brighter moments. "How are you getting one?" I wanted to know. "Living all right?"

"All right," she answered. I still couldn't get over the fact that she wasn't as talkative as she had been, that her voice was softer and flatter, with no more bite in it. But perhaps she felt strange at seeing me in the old house again after all this time, with everything just as she'd left it. I had a wireless now, that was the only difference.

"Got a job?" I asked. She seemed afraid to take the chair I'd offered her.

"At Hoskins," she told me, "on Ambergate. The lace factory. It pays forty-two bob a week, which isn't bad." She sat down and did up the remaining button of her coat. I saw she was looking at the fishing-boat picture again. The last of the fleet.

"It ain't good either. They never paid owt but starvation wages and never will I suppose. Where are you living, Kathy?"

Straightening her hair—a trace of grey near the roots—she said: "I've got a house at Sneinton. Little, but it's only seven and six a week. It's noisy as well, but I like it that way. I was always one for a bit of life, you know that. 'A pint of beer and a quart of noise' was what you used to say, didn't you?"

I smiled. "Fancy you remembering that." But she didn't look as though she had much of a life. Her eyes lacked that spark of humour that often soared up into the bonfire of a laugh. The lines around them now served only as an indication of age and passing time. "I'm glad to hear you're taking care of yourself."

She met my eyes for the first time. "You was never very excitable, was you, Harry?"

"No," I replied truthfully, "not all that much."

"You should have been," she said, though in an empty

sort of way, "then we might have hit it off a bit better."

"Too late now," I put in, getting the full blow-through of my words. "I was never one for rows and trouble, you know that. Peace is more my line."

She made a joke at which we both laughed. "Like that bloke Chamberlain!*"—then moved a plate to the middle of the table and laid her elbows on the cloth. "I've been looking after myself for the last three years."

It may be one of my faults, but I get a bit curious sometimes. "What's happened to that housepainter of yours then?" I asked this question quite naturally though, because I didn't feel I had anything to reproach her with. She'd gone away, and that was that. She hadn't left me in the lurch with a mountain of debts or any such thing. I'd always let her do what she liked.

"I see you've got a lot of books," she remarked, noticing one propped against the sauce bottle, and two more on the sideboard.

"They pass the time on," I replied, striking a match because my pipe had gone out. "I like reading."

She didn't say anything for a while. Three minutes I remember, because I was looking across at the clock on the dresser. The news would have been on the wireless, and I'd missed the best part of it. It was getting interesting because of the coming war. I didn't have anything else to do but think this while I was waiting for her to speak. "He died of lead-poisoning," she told me. "He did suffer a lot, and he was only forty-two. They took him away to the hospital a week before he died."

I couldn't say I was sorry, though it was impossible to hold much against him. I just didn't know the chap. "I don't think I've got a fag in the place to offer you," I said, looking on the mantelpiece in case I might find one, though knowing I wouldn't. She moved when I passed her on my search, scraping her chair along the floor. "No, don't bother to shift. I can get by."

*Chamberlain was the British Prime Minister in the years just before the Second World War. He came back from a meeting with the Germans, saying he had gained "Peace in our time".

"It's all right," she said. "I've got some here"—feeling in her pocket and bringing out a crumpled five-packet. "Have one, Harry?"

"No thanks. I haven't smoked a fag in twenty years. You know that. Don't you remember how I started smoking a pipe? When we were courting. You gave me one once for my birthday and told me to start smoking it because it would make me look more distinguished! So I've smoked one ever since. I got used to it quick enough, and I like it now. I'd never be without it in fact."

As if it were yesterday! But maybe I was talking too much, for she seemed a bit nervous while lighting her fag. I don't know why it was, because she didn't need to be in my house. "You know, Harry," she began, looking at the fishing-boat picture, nodding her head towards it, "I'd like to have that" —as though she'd never wanted anything so much in her life.

"Not a bad picture, is it?" I remember saying. "It's nice to have pictures on the wall, not to look at especially, but they're company. Even when you're not looking at them you know they're there. But you can take it if you like."

"Do you mean that?" she asked, in such a tone that I felt sorry for her for the first time.

"Of course. Take it. I've got no use for it. In any case I can get another picture if I want one, or put a war map up." It was the only picture on that wall, except for the wedding photo on the sideboard below. But I didn't want to remind her of the wedding picture for fear it would bring back memories she didn't like. I hadn't kept it there for sentimental reasons, so perhaps I should have dished it. "Did you have any kids?"

"No," she said, as if not interested. "But I don't like taking your picture, and I'd rather not if you think all that much of it." We sat looking over each other's shoulder for a long time. I wondered what had happened during these ten years to make her talk so sadly about the picture. It was getting dark outside. Why didn't she shut up about it, just take the bloody thing? So I offered it to her again, and to settle the issue unhooked it, dusted the back with a cloth, wrapped it up in brown paper, and tied the parcel with the best post-office string. "There you are," I said, brushing the pots aside, laying it on the table at her elbows.

"You're very good to me, Harry."

"Good! I like that. What does a picture more or less in the house matter? And what does it mean to me, anyway?" I can see now that we were giving each other hard knocks in a way we'd never learned to do when living together. I switched on the electric light. As she seemed uneasy when it showed everything up clearly in the room, I offered to switch it off again.

"No, don't bother"—standing to pick up her parcel. "I think I'll be going now. Happen I'll see you some other time."

"Drop in whenever you feel like it." Why not? We weren't enemies. She undid two buttons of her coat, as though having them loose would make her look more at her ease and happy in her clothes, then waved to me. "So long."

"Good night, Kathy" It struck me that she hadn't smile or laughed once the whole time she'd been there, so I smiled to her as she turned for the door, and what came back wasn't the bare-faced cheeky grin I once knew, but a wry parting of the lips moving more for exercise than humor. She must have been through it, I thought, and she's above forty now.

So she went. But it didn't take me long to get back to my book.

A few mornings later I was walking up St. Ann's Well Road delivering letters. My round was taking a long time, for I had to stop at almost every shop. It was raining, a fair drizzle, and water rolled off my cape, soaking my trousers below the knees so that I was looking forward to a mug of tea back in the canteen and hoping they'd kept the stove going. If I hadn't been so late on my round I'd have dropped into a café for a cup.

I'd just taken a pack of letters into a grocer's and, coming out, saw the fishing-boat picture in the next-door pawnshop window, the one I'd given Kathy a few days ago. There was no mistaking it, leaning back against ancient spirit-levels, bladeless planes, rusty hammers, trowels, and a violin case with the strap broken. I recognised a chip in the gold-painted woodwork near the bottom left corner of its frame.

For half a minute I couldn't believe it, was unable to make out how it had got there, then saw the first day of my married life and a sideboard loaded with presents, prominent among them this surviving triplet of a picture looking at me from the wreckage of other lives. And here it is, I thought, come down to a bloody nothing. She must have sold it that night before going home, pawnshops always keeping open late on a Friday so that women could get their husbands' suits out of pop for the week-end. Or maybe she'd sold it this morning, and I was only half an hour behind her on my round. Must have been really hard up. Poor Kathy, I thought. Why hadn't she asked me to let her have a bob or two?

I didn't think much about what I was going to do next. I never do, but went inside and stood at the shop counter waiting for a grey-haired doddering skinflint to sort out the popped bundles of two thin-faced women hovering to make sure he knew they were pawning the best of stuff. I was impatient. The place stank of old clothes and mildewed junk after coming out of fresh rain, and besides I was later than ever now on my round. The canteen would be closed before I got back, and I'd miss my morning tea.

The old man shuffled over at last, his hand out. "Got any letters?"

"Nowt like that, feyther. I'd just like to have a look at that picture you've got in your window, the one with a ship on it." The women went out counting what few shillings he'd given them, stuffing pawn-tickets in their purses, and the old man came back carrying the picture as if it was worth five quid.

Shock told me she'd sold it right enough, but belief lagged a long way behind, so I looked at it well to make sure it really was the one. A price marked on the back wasn't plain enough to read. "How much do you want for it?"

"You can have it for four bob."

Generosity itself. But I'm not one for bargaining. I could have got it for less, but I'd rather pay an extra bob than go through five minutes of chinning. So I handed the money over, and said I'd call back for the picture later.

Four measly bob, I said to myself as I sloshed on through the rain. The robbing bastard. He must have given poor Kathy about one and six for it. Three pints of beer for the fishing-boat picture.

I don't know why, but I was expecting her to call again the following week. She came on Thursday, at the same time, and was dressed in the usual way: summer frock showing through her brown winter coat whose buttons she couldn't leave alone, telling me how nervous she was. She'd had a drink or two on her way, and before coming into the house stopped off at the lavatory outside. I'd been late back from work, and hadn't quite finished my tea, asked her if she could do with a cup. "I don't feel like it," came the answer. "I had one not long ago."

I emptied the coal scuttle on the fire. "Sit down nearer the warmth. It's a bit nippy tonight."

She agreed that it was, then looked up at the fishing-boat picture on the wall. I'd been waiting for this, wondered what she'd say when she did, but there was no surprise at seeing it back in the old place, which made me feel a bit disappointed. "I won't be staying long tonight," was all she said. "I've got to see somebody at eight."

Not a word about the picture. "That's all right. How's your work going?"

"Putrid," she answered nonchalantly, as though my question had been out of place. "I got the sack, for telling the forewoman where to get off."

"Oh," I said, getting always to say "Oh" when I wanted to hide my feelings, though it was a safe bet that whenever I did say "Oh" there wasn't much else to come out with.

I had an idea she might want to live in my house again seeing she'd lost her job. If she wanted to she could. And she wouldn't be afraid to ask, even now. But I wasn't going to mention it first. Maybe that was my mistake, though I'll never know. "A pity you got the sack," I put in.

Her eyes were on the picture again, until she asked: "Can you lend me half-a-crown?"

"Of course I can"—emptied my trouser pocket, sorted out half-a-crown, and passed it across to her. Five pints. She couldn't think of anything to say, shuffled her feet to some soundless tune in her mind. "Thanks very much."

"Don't mention it," I said with a smile. I remembered buying a packet of fags in case she'd want one, which shows how much I'd expected her back. "Have a smoke?"—and she took one, struck a match on the sole of her shoe before I could get her a light myself.

"I'll give you the half-crown next week, when I get paid." That's funny, I thought. "I got a job as soon as I lost the other one," she added, reading my mind before I had time to speak. "It didn't take long. There's plenty of war work now. Better money as well."

"I suppose all the firms'll be changing over soon." It occurred to me that she could claim some sort of allowance from me—for we were still legally married—instead of coming to borrow half-a-crown. It was her right, and I didn't need to remind her; I wouldn't be all that much put out if she took me up on it. I'd been single—as you might say—for so many years that I hadn't been able to stop myself putting a few quid by. "I'll be going now," she said, standing up to fasten her coat.

"Sure you won't have a cup of tea?"

"No thanks. Want to catch the trolley back to Sneinton." I said I'd show her to the door. "Don't bother. I'll be all right." She stood waiting for me, looking at the picture on the wall above the sideboard. "It's a nice picture you've got up there. I always liked it a lot."

I made the old joke: "Yes, but it's the last of the fleet."

"That's why I like it." Not a word about having sold it for eighteen pence.

I showed her out, mystified.

She came to see me every week, all through the war, always on Thursday night at about the same time. We talked a bit, about the weather, the war, her job and my job, never anything important. Often we'd sit for a long time looking into the fire from our different stations in the room, me by the hearth and Kathy a bit further away at the table as if she'd just finished a meal, both of us silent yet not uneasy in it. Sometimes I made a cup of tea, sometimes not. I suppose now that I think of it I could have got a pint of beer in for when she came, but it never occurred to me. Not that I think she felt the lack of it, for it wasn't the sort of thing she expected to see in my house anyway.

She never missed coming once, even though she often had a cold in the winter and would have been better off in bed. The blackout and shrapnel didn't stop her either. In a quiet off-handed sort of way we got to enjoy ourselves and looked forward to seeing each other again, and maybe they were the best times we ever had together in our lives. They certainly helped us through the long monotonous dead evenings of the war.

She was always dressed in the same brown coat, growing shabbier and shabbier. And she wouldn't leave without borrowing a few shillings. Stood up: "Er . . . lend's half-a-dollar, Harry." Given, sometimes with a joke: "Don't get too drunk on it, will you?"—never responded to, as if it were bad manners to joke about a thing like that. I didn't get anything back of course, but then, I didn't miss such a dole either. So I wouldn't say no when she asked me, and as the price of beer went up she increased the amount to three bob then to three-and-six and, finally, just before she died, to four bob. It was a pleasure to be able to help her. Besides, I told myself, she has no one else. I never asked questions as to where she was living, though she did mention a time or two that it was still up Sneinton way. Neither did I at any time see her outside at a pub or picture house; Nottingham is a big town in many ways.

On every visit she would glance from time to time at the fishing-boat picture, the last of the fleet, hanging on the wall above the sideboard. She often mentioned how beautiful she thought it was, and how I should never part with it, how the sunrise and the ship and the woman and the sea were just right. Then a few minutes later she'd hint to me how nice it would be if she had it, but knowing it would end up in the pawnshop I didn't take her hints. I'd rather have lent her five bob instead of half-a-crown so that she wouldn't take the picture, but she never seemed to want more than half-a-crown in those first years. I once mentioned to her she could have more if she liked, but she didn't answer me. I don't think she wanted the picture especially to sell and get money, or to hang in her own house; only to have the pleasure of pawning it, to have someone else buy it so that it wouldn't belong to either of us any more.

But she finally did ask me directly, and I saw no reason to refuse when she put it like that. Just as I had done six years before, when she first came to see me, I dusted it, wrapped it up carefully in several layers of brown paper, tied it with post-office string, and gave it to her. She seemed happy with it under her arm, couldn't get out of the house quick enough, it seemed.

It was the same old story though, for a few days later I saw it again in the pawnshop window, among all the old junk that had been there for years. This time I didn't go in and try to get it back. In a way I wish I had, because then Kathy might not have had the accident that came a few days later. Though you never know. If it hadn't been that, it would have been something else.

I didn't get to her before she died. She'd been run down by a lorry at six o'clock in the evening, and by the time the police had taken me to the General Hospital she was dead. She'd been knocked all to bits, and had practically bled to death even before they'd got her to the hospital. The doctor told me she'd not been quite sober when she was knocked down. Among the things of hers they showed me was the fishing-boat picture, but it was so broken up and smeared with blood that I hardly recognised it. I burned it in the roaring flames of the firegrate late that night.

When her two brothers, their wives and children had left and taken with them the air of blame they attached to me for Kathy's accident I stood at the graveside thinking I was alone, hoping I would end up crying my eyes out. No such luck. Holding my head up suddenly I noticed a man

I hadn't seen before. It was a sunny afternoon of winter, but bitter cold, and the only thing at first able to take my mind off Kathy was the thought of some poor bloke having to break the bone-hard soil and dig this hole she was now lying in. Now there was this stranger. Tears were running down his cheeks, a man in his middle fifties wearing a good suit, grey though but with a black band around his arm, who moved only when the fedup sexton touched his shoulder—and then mine—to say it was all over.

I felt no need to ask who he was. And I was right. When I got to Kathy's house (it had also been his) he was packing his things, and left a while later in a taxi without saying a word. But the neighbours, who always know everything, told me he and Kathy had been living together for the last six years. Would you believe it? I only wished he'd made her happier than she'd been.

Time has passed now and I haven't bothered to get another picture for the wall. Maybe a war map would do it; the wall gets too blank, for I'm sure some government will oblige soon. But it doesn't really need anything at the moment, to tell you the truth. That part of the room is filled up by the sideboard, on which is still the wedding picture, that she never thought to ask for.

And looking at these few old pictures stacked in the back of my mind I began to realise that I should never have let them go, and that I shouldn't have let Kathy go either. Something told me I'd been daft and dead to do it, and as my rotten luck would have it it was the word dead more than daft that stuck in my mind, and still sticks there like the spinebone of a cod or conger eel, driving me potty sometimes when I lay of a night in bed thinking.

I began to believe there was no point in my life—became even too far gone to turn religious or go on the booze. Why had I lived? I wondered. I can't see anything for it. What was the point of it all? And yet at the worst minutes of my midnight emptiness I'd think less of myself and more of Kathy, see her as suffering in a far rottener way than ever I'd done, and it would come to me—though working only as long as an aspirin pitted against an incurable headache—that the object of my having been alive was that in some small way I'd helped Kathy through her life.

I was born dead, I kept telling myself. Everybody's dead, I answer. So they are, I maintain, but then most of them never know it like I'm beginning to do, and it's a bloody shame that this has come to me at last when I could least do with it, and when it's too bloody late to get anything but bad from it.

Then optimism rides out of the darkness like a knight in armour. If you loved her . . . (of course I bloody-well did) . . . then you both did the only thing possible if it was to be remembered as love. Now didn't you? Knight in armour goes back into blackness. Yes, I cry, but neither of us *did anything about it*, and that's the trouble.

The Decline and Fall of Frankie Buller

Sitting in what has come to be called my study, a room in the first-floor flat of a ramshackle Majorcan house, my eyes move over racks of books around me. Row after row of coloured backs and dusty tops, they give an air of distinction not only to the room but to the whole flat, and one can sense the thoughts of occasional visitors who stoop down discreetly during drinks to read their titles:

"A Greek lexicon, Homer in the original. He knows Greeks! (Wrong, those books belong to my brother-in-law.) Shakespeare, The Golden Bough, a Holy Bible bookmarked with tapes and paper. He even reads it! Euripides and the rest, and a dozen mouldering Baedekers. What a funny idea to collect them! Proust all twelve volumes! I never could wade through that lot. (Neither did I.) Dostoevsky. My God, is *he* still going strong?"

And so on and so on, items that have become part of me, foliage that has grown to conceal the bare stem of my real personality, what I was like before I ever saw these books, or any book at all, come to that. Often I would like to rip them away from me one by one, extract their shadows out of my mouth and heart, cut them neatly with a scalpel from my jungle-brain. Impossible. You can't wind back the clock that sits grinning on the marble shelf. You can't even smash its face in and forget it.

Yesterday we visited the house of a friend who lives further along the valley, away from the town noises so that sitting on the terrace with eyes half-closed and my head leaning back in a deck-chair, beneath a tree of half-ripe medlars and with the smell of plundered oranges still on my hands, I heard the sound of a cuckoo coming from the pine woods on the mountain slopes.

The cuckoo accomplished what a surgeon's knife could not. I was plunged back deep through the years into my natural state, without books and without the knowledge that I am supposed to have gained from them. I was suddenly landed beyond all immediate horizons of the past by the soft, sharp, fluting whistle of the cuckoo, and set down once more within the kingdom of Frankie Buller.

We were marching to war, and I was part of his army, with an elderberry stick at the slope and my pockets heavy with smooth, flat, well-chosen stones that would skim softly and swiftly through the air, and strike the foreheads of enemies. My plimsoll shoes were sprouting bunions, and there must have been a patch at the back of my trousers and holes in my socks, because I can never remember a time when there weren't, up to the age of fourteen.

The roll-call revealed eleven of us, yet Frankie was a full-blown centurion with his six-foot spear-headed railing at the slope, and his rusty dustbin lid for a shield. To make our numbers look huge to an enemy he marched us down from the bridge and across the field in twos, for Frankie was a good tactician, having led the local armies since he was fifteen years old.

At that time his age must have stood between twenty and twenty-five. Nobody seemed to know for sure, Frankie least of all, and it was supposed that his parents found it politic to keep the secret closely. When we asked Frankie how old he was he answered with the highly improbable number of: "'Undred an' fifty-eight." This reply was logically followed by another question: "When did you leave school then?" Sometimes he would retort scornfully to this "I never went to school." Or he might answer with a proud, grin: "I didn't leave, I ran away."

I wore short trousers, and he wore long trousers, so it was impossible for me to say how tall he was in feet and inches. In appearance he seemed like a giant. He had grey eyes and dark hair, and regular features that would have made him passably handsome had not a subtle air of pre-pubescent unreliability lurked in his eyes and around the lines of his low brow. In body and strength he lacked nothing for a full-grown man.

We in the ranks automatically gave him the title of General, but he insisted on being addressed as Sergeant-Major, because his father had been a sergeant-major in the First World War. "My dad was wounded in the war," he told us every time we saw him. "He got a medal and shell-shock, and because he got shell-shock, that's why I'm like I am."

He was glad and proud of being "like he was" because it meant he did not have to work in a factory all day and earn his living like other men of his age. He preferred to lead the gang of twelve-year-olds in our street to war against the same age group of another district. Our street was a straggling line of ancient back-to-backs on the city's edge, while the enemy district was a new housing estate of three long streets which had outflanked us and left us a mere pocket of country in which to run wild—a few fields and allotment gardens, which was reason enough for holding an eternal grudge against them. People from the slums in the city-centre lived in the housing estate, so that our enemies were no less ferocious than we, except that they didn't have a twenty-year-old backward youth like Frankie to lead them into battle. The inhabitants of the housing estate had not discarded their slum habits, so that the area became known to our street as "Sodom".

"We're goin' ter raid Sodom today," Frankie said, when we were lined-up on parade. He did not know the Biblical association* of the word, thinking it a name officially given by the city council.

So we walked down the street in twos and threes, and formed up on the bridge over the River Lean. Frankie would order us to surround any stray children we met with on the way, and if they wouldn't willingly fall in with us as recruits he would follow one of three courses. First: he might have them bound with a piece of clothes-line and brought with us by force; second: threaten to torture them until they agreed to come with us of their own free will; third: bat them

*In the Bible the city of Sodom is described as being so wicked that it was destroyed by fire from heaven.

across the head with his formidable hand and send them home weeping, or snarling back curses at him from a safe distance. I had come to join his gang through clause number two, and had stayed with it for profitable reasons of fun and adventure. My father often said: "If I see yo' gooin' about wi' that daft Frankie Buller I'll clink yer tab-'ole."

Although Frankie was often in trouble with the police he could never, even disregarding his age, be accurately described as a "juvenile delinquent". He was threatened regularly by the law with being sent to borstal, but his antics did not claim for him a higher categorical glory than that of "general nuisance" and so kept him out of the clutches of such institutions. His father drew a pension due to wounds from the war, and his mother worked at the tobacco factory, and on this combined income the three of them seemed to live at a higher standard than the rest of us, whose fathers were permanent appendages at the dole office. The fact that Frankie was an only child in a district where some families numbered up to half a dozen was accounted for by the rumour that the father, having seen Frankie at birth, had decided to run no more risks. Another whispered reason concerned the nature of Mr. Buller's pensionable wound.

We used to ask Frankie, when we made camp in the woods and squatted around a fire roasting plundered potatoes after victory, what he was going to do when the Second War started.

"Join up," he would say, non-committally.

"What in, Frankie?" someone would ask respectfully, for Frankie's age and strength counted for much more than the fact that the rest of us knew roughly how to read and write.

Frankie responded by hurling a piece of wood at his interrogator. He was a crackshot at any kind of throw, and rarely missed hitting the shoulder or chest. "Yer've got to call me 'SIR'!" he roared, his arms trembling with rightful anger. "Yer can get out to the edge of the wood and keep guard for that." The bruised culprit slunk off through the bushes, clutching his pole and stones.

"What would you join, sir?" a more knowing ranker said.

Such respect made him amiable:

"The Sherwood Foresters. That's the regiment my dad

was in. He got a medal in France for killin' sixty-three Jerries in one day. He was in a dug-out, see"—Frankie could act this with powerful realism since seeing *All Quiet on the Western Front* and *The Lives of a Bengal Lancer*—"behind his machine gun, and the Jerries come over at dawn, and my dad seed 'em and started shootin'. They kept comin' over, but the Old Man just kept on firin' away—der-der-der-der-der-der-der—even when all his pals was dead. My old Man was 'it with a bullet as well, but 'e din't let go of 'is gun, and the Jerries was fallin' dead like flies, dropping all round 'im, and when the rest o' the Sherwoods came back to 'elp 'im and stop the Jerries coming over, 'e counted sixty-three dead bodies in front on 'is gun. So they gen 'im a medal and sent 'im back ter England."

He looked around at the semicircle of us. "What do yer think o' that, then?" he demanded savagely, as if he himself were the hero and we were disputing it. "All right," he ordered, when we had given the required appreciation to his father's exploits, "I want yer all ter scout round for wood so's the fire wain't goo out."

Frankie was passionately interested in war. He would often slip a penny into my hand and tell me to fetch an *Evening Post* so that I could read to him the latest war news from China, Abyssinia, or Spain, and he would lean against the wall of his house, his grey eyes gazing at the roofs across the street, saying whenever I stopped for breath: "Go on, Alan, read me a bit more. Read me that bit about Madrid again. . . ."

Frankie was a colossus, yet a brave man who formed us up and laid us in the hollows of a field facing the railway embankment that defended the approaches to the streets of Sodom. We would wait for an hour, a dozen of us with faces pressed to the earth, feeling our sticks and trying to stop the stones in our pockets from rattling. If anyone stirred Frankie would whisper out a threat: "The next man to move, I'll smash 'im with my knobkerrie*."

We were three hundred yards from the embankment. The grass beneath us was smooth and sweet, and Frankie chewed it by the mouthful, stipulating that no one else must do

*short, thick stick, with a knobbled end used as a weapon.

so because it was worse than Deadly Nightshade. It would kill us in five second flat if we were to eat it, he went on, but it would do him no harm because he was proof against poison of all kinds. There was magic inside him that would not let it kill him; he was a witch doctor, and, for anyone who wasn't, the grass would scorch his guts away.

An express train came out of the station, gathered speed on the bend, and blocked the pink eavings of Sodom from view while we lifted our heads from the grass and counted the carriages. Then we saw our enemies, several figures standing on the railway tracks, brandishing sticks and throwing stones with playful viciousness into a pool of water down the slope.

"It's the Sodom gang," we whispered.

"Keep quiet," Frankie hissed. "How many do you see?"

"Can't tell."

"Eight."

"There's more comin' up."

"Pretend they're Germans," Frankie said.

They came down the slope and, one by one, lifted themselves over to our side of the railings. On the embankment they shouted and called out to each other, but once in the field they walked close together without making much noise. I saw nine of them, with several more still boldly trespassing on the railway line. I remembered that we were eleven, and while waiting for the signal to rush forward I kept saying to myself: "It won't be long now. It can't be long now."

Frankie mumbled his final orders. "You lot go left. You other lot go right. We'll go in front. I want 'em surrounded." The only military triumph he recognized was to surround and capture.

He was on his feet, brandishing an iron spear and waving a shield. We stood up with him and, stretched out in a line, advanced slowly, throwing stones as fast as our arms would move into the concentric ring of the enemy gang.

It was a typical skirmish. Having no David to bring against our Goliath they slung a few ineffectual stones and ran back helter-skelter over the railings, mounting the slope to the railway line. Several of them were hit.

"Prisoners!" Frankie bellowed, but they bolted at the last moment and escaped. For some minutes stones flew between field and embankment, and our flanks were unable to push forward and surround. The enemy exulted then from the railway line because they had a harvest of specially laid stones between the tracks, while we had grass underfoot, with no prospect of finding more ammunition when our pockets were emptied. If they rallied and came back at us, we would have to retreat half a mile before finding stones at the bridge.

Frankie realised all this in a second. The same tactical situation had occurred before. Now some of us were hit. A few fell back. Someone's eye was cut. My head was streaming with blood, but I disregarded this for the moment because I was more afraid of the good hiding I would catch from my father's meaty fist at home for getting into a fight, than blood and a little pain. ("Yer've bin wi' that Frankie Buller agen, ain't yer?" Bump. "What did I tell yer? Not ter ger wi' 'im, din't I?" Bump. "And yer don't do what I tell yer, do you?" Bump. "Yer'll keep on gooin' wi' that Frankie Buller tell yer as daft as 'e is, wain't yer?" Bump-Bump.)

We were wavering. My pockets were light and almost empty of stones. My arms ached with flinging them.

"All right if we charge, lads?" Frankie called out.

There was only one answer to his words. We were with him, right into the ovens of a furnace had he asked it. Perhaps he led us into these bad situations, in which no retreat was possible, just for the fine feeling of a glorious win or lose.

"Yes!" we all shouted together.

"Come on, then," he bawled out at the top of his voice: "CHARGE!"

His great strides carried him the hundred yards in a few seconds, and he was already climbing the railing. Stones from the Sodom lot were clanging and rattling against his shield. Lacking the emblematic spear and dustbin lid of a leader we went forward more slowly, aiming our last stones at the gang on the embankment above.

As we mounted the railings on his left and right Frankie was half-way up the slope, within a few yards of the enemy. He exhorted his wings all the time to make more speed and surround them, waving his dangerous spear-headed length of iron now before their faces. From lagging slightly we suddenly swept in on both flanks, reaching the railway line in one rush to replenish our stocks of ammunition, while Frankie went on belabouring them from the front.

They broke, and ran down the other slope, down into the streets of Sodom, scattering into the refuge of their rows of pink houses whose doors were already scratched and scarred, and where, it was rumoured, they kept coal in their bathrooms (though this was secretly envied by us as a commodious coal-scuttle so conveniently near to the kitchen) and strung poaching nets out in their back gardens.

When the women of our street could think of no more bad names to call Frankie Buller for leading their children into fights that resulted in black eyes, torn clothes, and split heads, they called him a Zulu, a label that Frankie nevertheless came to accept as a tribute, regarding it as being synonymous with bravery and recklessness, "Why do you run around with that bleddy Zulu?" a mother demanded from her child as she tore up one of father's old shirts for a bandage or patch. And immediately there was conjured up before you Frankie, a wild figure wielding spear and dustbin lid, jumping up and down before leading his gang into battle. When prisoners were taken he would have them tied to a tree or fence-post, then order his gang to do a war dance around them. After the performance, in which he in his fierce panoply sometimes took part, he would have a fire built near by and shout out that he was going to have the prisoners tortured to death now. He once came so near to carrying out this threat that one of us ran back and persuaded Frankie's father to come and deal with his son and set the prisoners free. And so Mr. Buller and two other men, one of them my father, came striding down the steps of the bridge. They walked quickly across the field, short, stocky, black-browed Chris, and bald Buller with his walrus moustache. But the same person who had given the alarm crept back into Frankie's camp and gave warning there, so that when the three men arrived, ready to buckle Frankie down and drive him home, they found nothing except a kicked-out fire and a frightened but unharmed pair of captives still tied to a tree.

It was a fact that Frankie's acts of terrorism multiplied as the war drew nearer, though many of them passed unnoticed because of the preoccupied and brooding atmosphere of that summer. He would lead his gang into allotments and break into the huts, scattering tools and flower seeds with a maniacal energy around the garden, driving a lawnmower over lettuce-heads and parsley, leaving a litter of decapitated chrysanthemums in his track. His favourite sport was to stand outside one of the huts and throw his spear at it with such force that its iron barb ran right through the thin wood.

We had long since said farewell to the novelty of possessing gasmasks. Frankie led us on a foray over the fields one day, out on a raid with masks on our faces—having sworn that the white cloud above the wood was filled with mustard gas let loose from the Jerry trenches on the other side—and they became so broken up in the scuffle that we threw each one ceremoniously into a fire before going home, preferring to say we had lost them rather than show the tattered relics that remained.

So many windows were broken, dustbins upturned, air let out of bicycle tyres, and heads split as a result of Pyrrhic victories in gang raids—for he seemed suddenly to be losing his military genius—that it became dangerous for Frankie to walk down our street. Stuffing a few shreds of tobacco into one of his father's old pipes—tobacco that we collected for him as cigarette-ends—he would walk along the middle of the street, and suddenly an irate woman would rush out of an entry wielding a clothes-prop and start frantically hitting him.

"I saw you empty my dustbin last night, you bleddy Zulu, you grett daft baby. Take that, and that, and that!"

"It worn't me, missis. I swear to God it worn't," he

would shout in protest, arms folded over his head and galloping away to avoid her blows.

"Yo' come near my house agen," she shouted after him, "and I'll cool yer down wi' a bucket o' water, yo' see'f I don't."

Out of range, he looked back at her, bewildered, angry, his blood boiling with resentment. He shouted out the worst swear-words he knew, and disappeared into his house, slamming the door behind him.

It was not only the outbreak of the war that caused Frankie's downfall. Partly it came about because there was a romantic side to his nature that evinced itself in other means than mock warfare. At the end of many afternoons in the summer he stood at the top of our street and waited for the girls to come out of the tobacco factory. Two thousand worked there, and about a quarter of them passed by every evening on their way home to tea.

He mostly stood there alone in his black corduroy trousers, patched jacket, and a collarless shirt belonging to his father, but if an older member of the gang stayed for company it by no means inhibited his particular brand of courtship. He had the loudest mouth-whistle in the street, and this was put to good and musical use as the girls went by with arms linked in twos and threes.

"Hey up, duck!" he would call out. "How are yer?"

A shrug of the shoulders, a toss of the head, laughter, or a sharp retort came back.

"Can I tek yer out tonight?" he cried with a loud laugh. "Do you want me to treat you to't pictures?"

Occasionally a girl would cross to the other side of the road to avoid him, and she would be singled out for his most special witticism:

"Hey up good-lookin,' can I cum up and see yer some time?"

Responses flew back like this, laced around with much laughter:

"It'll cost yer five quid!"

"Ye'r daft, me duck, yer foller balloons!"

"I'll meet you at the Grand at eight. Don't forget to be there, because I shall!"

It was his greatest hour of mature diversion. He was merely acting his age, following, though in a much exaggerated manner, what the other twenty-year-olds did in the district. The consummation of these unique courtships took place among the bulrushes, in the marsh between the River Lean and the railway line where Frankie rarely led his gang. He stalked alone (a whistled-at girl accompanying him only as a dim picture in his mind) along concealed paths to catch tadpoles and then to lie by himself in a secret place where no one could see him, self-styled boss of osiers, elderberry and bordering oak. From which journey he returned pale and shifty-eyed with guilt and a pleasurable memory.

He stood at the street corner every evening as the summer wore on, at first with many of the gang, but later alone because his remarks to the passing factory girls were no longer innocent, so that one evening a policeman came and drove him away from the street corner for ever. During those same months hundreds of loaded lorries went day after day to the edge of the marsh and dumped rubble there, until Frankie's secret hiding place was obliterated, and above it lay the firm foundation for another branch of the tobacco factory.

On the Sunday morning that my mother and father shook their heads over Chamberlain's melancholy voice issuing from the webbed heart-shaped speaker of our wireless set, I met Frankie in the street.

I asked what he would do now there was a war on, for I assumed that in view of his conscriptable age he would be called-up with the rest of the world. He seemed inert and sad, and I took this to be because of the war, a mask of proper seriousness that should be on everybody's face, even though I didn't feel it to be on my own. I also noticed that when he spoke he did so with a stammer. He sat on the pavement with his back leaning against the wall of some house, instinctively knowing that no one would think of pummelling him with a clothes-prop today.

"I'll just wait for my calling-up papers," he answered. "Then I'll get in the Sherwood Foresters."

"If I get called-up I'll go in the navy," I put in, when he did not offer an anecdote about his father's exploits in the last war.

"The army's the only thing to join, Alan," he said with deep conviction, standing up and taking out his pipe.

He suddenly smiled, his dejection gone. "I'll tell you what, after dinner we'll get the gang together and go over New Bridge for manoeuvres. I've got to get you all into shape now there's a war on. We'll do a bit o' training. P'raps we'll meet some o' the Sodom lot."

As we marched along that afternoon Frankie outlined his plan for our future. When we were about sixteen, he said, if the war was still on—it was bound to be because the Germans were tough, his old man told him so, though they wouldn't win in the end because their officers always sent the men over the top first—he'd take us down to the recruiting depot in town and enlist us together, all at the same time. In that way he—Frankie—would be our platoon commander.

It was a wonderful idea. All hands were thrust into the air.

The field was clear over New Bridge. We stood in a line along the parapet and saw without comment the newest proof of the city's advance. The grazing lands and allotments were now cut off from the main spread of the countryside by a boulevard sprouting from Sodom's new houses, with cars and Corporation double-deckers already running along it.

There was no sign of the Sodom lot, so Frankie ordered three of us to disappear into the gullies and hollows for the rest of the gang to track down. The next item on the training programme was target practice, a tin can set on a tree trunk until it was knocked over with stones from fifty yards. After fencing lessons and wrestling matches six of the Sodom gang appeared on the railway line, and at the end of a quick brutal skirmish they were held fast as prisoners. Frankie wished neither to keep them nor harm them, and let them go after making them swear an oath of allegiance to the Sherwood Foresters.

At seven o'clock we were formed up in double file to be marched back. Someone grumbled that it was a late hour to get home to tea, and for once Frankie succumbed to what I clearly remembered seeing as insubordination. He listened to the complaint and decided to cut our journey short by leading us across the branch-line that ran into the colliery. The factories and squalid streets on the hill had turned a sombre ochred colour, as if storm would burst during the night, and the clouds above the city were pink giving an unreal impression of profound silence so that we felt exposed, as if the railwayman in the distant signal box could see us and hear every word we spoke.

One by one we climbed the wire fence, Frankie crouching in the bushes and telling us when he thought the path was clear. He sent us over one at a time, and we leapt the six tracks yet kept our backs bent, as if we were passing a machine-gun post. Between the last line and the fence stood an obstacle in the form of a grounded railway carriage that served as a repair and tool-storage shed. Frankie had assured us that no one was in it, but when we were all across, the others already rushing through the field and up on to the lane, I turned around and saw a railwayman come out of the door and stop Frankie just as he was making for the fence.

I didn't hear any distinct words only the muffled sound of arguing. I kept down between the osiers and watched the railwayman poking his finger at Frankie's chest as if he were giving him some really strong advice. Then Frankie began to wave his hands in the air, as though he could not tolerate being stopped in this way, with his whole gang looking on from the field, as he thought.

Then, in one vivid second, I saw Frankie snatch a pint bottle from his jacket pocket and hit the railwayman over the head with it. In the exaggerated silence I heard the crash, and a cry of shock, rage, and pain from the man. Frankie then turned and ran in my direction, leaping like a zebra over the fence. When he drew level and saw me he cried wildly:

"Run, Alan, run. He asked for it. He asked for it."

And we ran.

The next day my brothers, sisters and myself were loaded into Corporation buses and transported to Workshop. We were evacuated, our few belongings thrust into paper carrier-bags, away from the expected bombs, along with most other children of the city. In one fatal blow Frankie's gang was taken away from him, and Frankie himself was carried off to the police station for hitting the railwayman on the head with a bottle. He was also charged with trespassing.

It may have been that the beginning of the war coincided with the end of Frankie's so-called adolescence, though ever after traces of it frequently appeared in his behaviour. For instance he would still tramp from one end of the city to the other, even through smokescreen and blackout, in the hope of finding some cinema that showed a good cowboy film.

I didn't meet Frankie again for two years. One day I saw a man pushing a handcart up the old street in which we did not live any more. The man was Frankie, and the handcart was loaded with bundles of wood, the sort of kindling that housewives spread over a crumpled-up *Evening Post* before making a morning fire. We couldn't find much to talk about, and Frankie seemed condescending in his attitude to me, as though ashamed to be seen talking to one so much younger than himself. This was not obvious in any plain way, yet I felt it and, being thirteen, resented it. Times had definitely altered. We just weren't pals any more. I tried to break once again into the atmosphere of old times by saying:

"Did you try to get into the army then, Frankie?"

I realise now that it was an indiscreet thing to say, and might have hurt him. I did not notice it then, yet I remembered his sensitivity as he answered:

"What do you mean? I *am* in the army. I joined-up

a year ago. The old man's back in the army as well—sergeany-major—and I'm in 'is cumpny."

The conversation quickly ended. Frankie pushed his barrow to the next entry, and began unloading his bundles of wood.

I didn't meet him for more than ten years. In that time I too had done my "sodjerin'", in Malaya, and I had forgotten the childish games we used to play with Frankie Buller, and the pitched battles with the Sodom lot over New Bridge.

I didn't live in the same city any more. I suppose it could be said that I had risen from the ranks. I had become a writer of sorts, having for some indescribable reason, after the evacuation and during the later bombs, taken to reading books.

I went back home to visit my family, and on my way through the streets about six o'clock one winter's evening, I heard someone call out:

"Alan!"

I recognised the voice instantly. I turned and saw Frankie standing before a cinema billboard, trying to read it. He was about thirty-five now, no longer the javelin-wielding colossus he once appeared, but nearer my own height, thinner, an unmistakable air of meekness in his face, almost respectable in his cap and black topcoat with white muffler tucked neatly inside. I noticed the green medal-ribbon on the lapel of his coat, and that confirmed what I had heard about him from time to time during the last ten years. From being the sergeant-major of our gang he had become a private soldier in the Home Guard, a runner indeed in his father's company. With tin-hat on his sweating low-browed head Frankie had stalked with messages through country whose every blade of grass he knew.

He was not my leader any more, and we both instantly recognised the fact as we shook hands. Frankie's one-man wood business had prospered and he now went around the streets with a pony and cart. He wasn't well-off, but he was his own employer. The outspoken ambition of our class was to become one's own boss. He knew he wasn't the leader of kindred spirits any more, while he probably wondered as we spoke whether or not I might be, which could have accounted for his shyness.

Not only had we both grown up in our different ways since the days when with dustbin lid and railing-spear he led his battalion into pitiless stone-throwing forays, but something of which I did not know had happened to him. Coming from the same class and, one might say, from the same childhood, there should have been some tree-root of recognition between us, despite the fact that our outer foliage of leaves would have wilted somewhat before each other's differing shade and colour. But there was no contact and I, being possessed of what the world I had moved into often termed "heightened consciousness", knew that it was due as much to something in Frankie as in me.

" 'Ow are yer gooin' on these days, Frankie?" I asked, revelling in the old accent, though knowing that I no longer had the right to use it.

His stammer was just short of what we would once have derisively called a stutter. "All right now. I feel a lot better, after that year I had in hospital."

I looked him quickly and discreetly up and down for evidence of a lame foot, a broken limb, a scar: for why else did people go to hospital? "What were you in for?" I asked.

In replying, his stammer increased. I felt he hesitated because for one moment he did not know which tone to take, though the final voice he used was almost proud, and certainly serious. "Shock treatment. That's why I went."

"What did they give you shock treatment for, Frankie?" I asked this question calmly, genuinely unable to comprehend what he told me, until the full horrible details of what Frankie must have undergone flashed into my mind. And then I wanted power in me to tear down those white-smocked mad interferers with Frankie's coal-forest world, wanted to wipe out their hate and presumption.

He pulled his coat collar up because, in the dusk, it was beginning to rain. "Well, you see, Alan," he began, with what I recognised now as a responsible and conforming face, "I had a fight with the Old Man, and after it, I blacked out. I hurt my dad, and he sent for the police. They fetched a doctor, and the doctor said I'd have to go to the hospital." They had even taught him to call it "Hospital". In the old days he would have roared with laughter and said:

" 'Sylum!"

"I'm glad you're better now, then," I said, and during the long pause that followed I realised that Frankie's world was after all untouchable, that the conscientious-scientific-methodical probers could no doubt reach it, could drive it into hiding, could kill the physical body that housed it, but had no power in the long run really to harm such minds. There is a part of the jungle that the scalpel can never reach.

He wanted to go. The rain was worrying him. Then, remembered why he had called me over, he turned to face the broad black lettering on a yellow background. "Is that for the Savoy?" he asked, nodding at the poster.

"Yes," I said.

He explained apologetically: "I forgot me glasses, Alan. Can you read it for me, and tell me what's on tonight."

"Sure, Frankie" I read it out: "Gary Cooper, in *Saratoga Trunk*."

I wonder if it's any good?" he asked. "Do you think it's a cowboy picture, or a love picture?"

I was able to help him on this point. I wondered, after the shock treatment, which of these subjects he would prefer. Intc what circle of his dark, devil-populated world had the jolts of electricity penetrated? "I've seen that picture before," I told him. "It's a sort of cowboy picture. There's a terrific train smash at the end."

Then I saw. I think he was surprised that I shock his hand so firmly when we parted. My explanation of the picture's main points acted on him like a charm. Into his eyes came the same glint I has seen years ago when he stood up with spear and shield and roared out: "CHARGE!" and flung himself against showers of sticks and flying stones.

"It sounds good," he said. "That's the picture for me. I's'll see that."

He pulled his cap lower down, made sure that his coat-collar covered his throat and neck, and walked with stirred imagination off into the driving rain.

"Cheerio, Frank," I called out as he turned the corner. I wondered what would be left of him by the time they had finished. Would they succeed in tapping and draining dry the immense subterranean reservoir of his dark inspired mind?

I watched him. He ignored the traffic-lights, walked diagonally across the wide wet road, then ran after a bus and leapt safely on to its empty platform.

And I with my books have not seen him since. It was like saying goodbye to a big part of me, for ever.

The Author's Introduction

I recently read some of my poems at a public reading, in the company of three other poets, and at the end of the session people from the audience were invited to ask questions about our work. One restive person considered that my poems were neither very plain nor straightforward, and asked whether or not I thought it was the poet's—or indeed the writer's—duty to communicate with people.

Now the idea "to communicate" has always seemed to me a suspicious concept, somewhat frightening because it often appears to contain a threat to the freedom of the writer. Still, the question had been asked, and as I was on a public platform it had somehow to be answered. To communicate with whom? I wondered. And with what object? It was something I hadn't much thought about before.

The only answer I could give, with which I hoped to satisfy both the questioner and myself, was to say that when I wrote, whether poetry or prose, my only desire was to communicate with myself. I didn't envisage certain groups of people reading my work while I was in the process of writing it. I didn't even think forward to when I would be reading it to myself after the first draft had been written. I went step by step, and none of them overlapped.

When I think of a story my only desire is to communicate the language and idea of it on to paper, to fix the muddled cloudiness of the incident by pen and ink so that it becomes clear, set down in plain English for me to read and reread and, with luck, for others to read later when it gets put into print and bound into a magazine or book.

If I have developed any skill or talent it is only to clarify the misty and occasionally musty vision of a face whose features are involved in some form of emotion, suffering in particular circumstances that force me to the act of recording them on the seismograph of my own mind. The face need not be one that is surfacing out of some far-off memory, may never have been seen or sensed but comes complete and strong out of the imagination (whatever that is: it may cover a multitude of sins for all I know) from I don't know where, or even out of a dream, some twisted drama neither fact nor fiction but instead a forked memory that my mother and father once had but that I never did and that they never told to me. A certain amount does nevertheless emerge from the reality that I call memory, or the actuality of hearsay, or a paragraph written in a trance for the novelty of its music and left idle for a year or so, or until such time as I see it again and use this paragraph as a springboard for pages and pages that wind into a story.

While on a visit to England in the spring of 1957 I stayed in a country cottage, and one afternoon, idly looking out of the window, I saw a man in white shorts and vest running by outside. He vanished around the bend of a tall hedge and headed towards a wood at the lane-end. I took out a blank sheet of foolscap and wrote on it a single sentence: The loneliness of the long-distance runner. Then I put the paper away and forgot all about it. A year later I was living in the Spanish seaport of Alicante, but had just given up my flat and was packing my things in order to come back to England. I was sorting through manuscripts and papers, throwing out much in order to lighten the suitcases. Then I saw this sheet of paper with "The loneliness of the long-distance runner" written along the top of it, and without bothering anymore about packing I wrote eight thousand words of the story which was given that title when finished, the other half being completed after I got to England.

All this is to say that what I write is a mixing of truth and untruth, plus the sort of barefaced tongue-in-the-cheek lies that make stories seem true to the bone. Life is all lies, truth is all lies, lies are all truth. The inability to distinguish truth from lies, to call nothing the truth, and call no lies lies, this is the basis of one's soul as a storyteller and spinner of picaresque novels.

The only truth is language, and that is the hardest truth of all for a writer to wield, and for a person to begin to understand if he or she is to become a writer. Writing in English is a great experience. It has a vast vocabulary, malleability, tortuousness, texture, colour. There is nothing hard or scientific about the English language. It is devious and beautiful and precise—qualities one tries to use as a blacksmith uses the tools of his strong and often subtle art. A writer is Saint George fighting and vanquishing the dragon of language in order to marry the princess of art. Whatever I write I read over to myself aloud in order to see how words coalesce and rhythm carries along the ideas and pictures clearer and more active rather than dulls them for the reader.

As I read it aloud I try not to get drugged and drunk by the flow and sound of my own voice, because I must be ice-cold and critical towards every phrase. If anything is easy it is bad. If anything is good I must suspect the seeds of failure in it—and root them out. It is not a matter of knowing how to spell, or being able to define the various components of English grammar, so much as being able to detect the final matching of truth and language. If it doesn't sound right, it is lies. If it does sound exactly right, as you can get it, then it is not necessarily the truth, but as close to it that you can attain during that particular moment.

I often need to write a story half a dozen times before I can consider it complete. Yet I know that nothing is ever complete, no more than a person's life can be. I don't imagine any dying man has ever thought his life complete, if of course he has the time or consciousness to reflect on this, that he still hadn't some work to do or problem to solve or even pleasure to taste. Part of one's art, though, is knowing when a story or novel is finalised, that a story in quality is as finished as you can make it, is at the proper apex of its form, and that if you go on working and tinkering with it you will begin to ease out any poetry and freshness that may have been there in the first place. I like to write stories, but not to ruin them. In a sense it is not true that I communicate only with myself when I write a story or novel or poem, but I certainly do when in the actual process of getting it through the broad nib of my pen onto paper.

The ideal story, I have always felt, is a narrative spoken aloud by an illiterate man to a group surrounding a fire in the forest at night, or told by a man to his friends in a pub, or at the table during dinner-hour in a canteen. I see such a story not as an incident which begins at point A and goes in a line thinly but straight to point B, but rather as a circuitous embellishment, twisting and convoluted, meandering all over the place until, near the end, these irrelevancies can at last be seen to have a point, and so can now come together on the main theme and climax.

In 1957 I was lent a book called *A Treasury of Yiddish Stories*, and in that volume I found the ideal model in a story called "Sand" by Israel Joshua Singer. There were many other stories too numerous to mention, beautifully and poetically told, but which seemed to be voiced, muttered and sometimes shouted rather than written—though they were indeed written. I had already turned off a few stories myself (e.g. "Uncle Ernest", "On Saturday Afternoon", "The Fishing-boat Picture") which seemed to fit this pattern though none of them had the deep colours of these Yiddish stories. I believe the actual form of *The Loneliness of the Long-Distance Runner* was based on a reading of this volume, though not of course consciously as I was writing it. A story is a separate re-creation of life that comes before you as you read, something ideally that obliterates your own life as you enter the act of reading it.

Few stories are as great as this. Apart from the one mentioned I think Joseph Conrad achieves this standard of genius in "The Heart of Darkness", as does Herman Melville in *Las Encantadas*, and Chekhov in "The Steppe". These are great stories, the greatest that the art of the short story can attain—or indeed that the art of writing can reach. Two of those mentioned were written by people who were not English, and Conrad was not born into the English language. Melville was American.

Perhaps English writers have taken the short story too seriously ever to have any great respect for it. Or perhaps they have tended to come from that stiff-upper-lip section of society that regards the monumental construction of novels as more in keeping with the ethic of output-materialism. They lack perhaps the immemorial tribal instinct of ghetto or village in which time does not exist, the ethos in which a story can be told with patience and understanding and love. For the story comes from those who crowd around bench or camp fire or street corner to listen, who move on to fresh pastures, or go back to work, or to a new town because they are harried by persecutions, and don't have much time to listen or, if they do, have not yet got into the habit or fields of literacy that will allow them to absorb novels.

Of the eight stories in the present volume only three were more or less based on actual events and people, and with these I shall deal first. "Noah's Ark" has no particular plot. Two boys set out to visit the Goose Fair in Nottingham, preferring the romance of engines and gay-painted caravans to the fictional romance of *Masterman Ready* which at its highest point of distraction is all that their school can offer them. They have fourpence to spend, and both know that they should forfeit this because at home their families have nothing with which to buy food. But it is not possible, for man does not live by bread alone, and neither do children. Even the half-starved must have fairs and circuses, and this is the only spiritual fare that the world can offer them at the particular age they are at.

The Goose Fair is common, raucous, and delightful, and later they beg for money, steal and cheat so as to extend the make-believe that can never be part of their lives. The pleasure-island of the brain and body spreads all around them, but beyond that island lies the mainland to which they must inevitably return, the continent of poverty and scarcity, parents continually quarrelling because they live during the 1930s in a land where millions of men have no work to do. So the two boys would do anything to spin out the experience of the fair for as long as possible.

"Uncle Ernest" is based upon a real person and a real incident. He was in fact my own uncle—an upholsterer by trade. As a young man he was called up to be a soldier in the First World War, but he repeatedly deserted from the army rather than be sent to the useless slaughter in France. For some weeks he was hiding in the woods outside Nottingham, and every day his mother cooked him a hot meal. It was my father's duty, who was then about fifteen, to take the food to him. One evening, unfortunately, he was followed by the militay police, who then apprehended Uncle Edgar (which was his real name). But he escaped again from the army, and came to Nottingham one night only to borrow a bicycle. At a family discussion it was decided that the best thing would be for him to go to a town near Coventry and live there unobtrusively with one of his married sisters. She and her husband, they knew, would look after him. My father was again called in to help. Two bicycles were procured, and his job was to guide Edgar almost from door to door by showing him the way along the towpaths of various canals—double the distance but twice as safe. They would certainly have been stopped at some point on the way if they had taken the normal main roads. The twisting convolutions of their journey could be likened in shape to the camp-fire stories already mentioned. What the two brothers said to each other, and how they passed the journey during the whole summer nights, is a story I have not yet written.

But Uncle Edgar, a pleasure-loving young man of twenty-three, was caught coming out of a cinema one night, and taken back into the army. After a short term of imprisonment (they needed cannon-fodder too badly for it to be very long) he was packed off to the Western Front where, at the first opportunity, he managed to be taken prisoner by the Germans—yet only after frightful experiences. But these years, of fighting against the authorities, whom he had reason to loath, and against the Germans, whom he had no particular reason to, unhinged him to the extent that he could never settle in society again. The way he lived from then on is depicted in my story. He was knocked down by a bus a few years ago, probably while drunk, and died some weeks later in hospital. Such was the life of Uncle Ernest.

I wrote the story in 1950 (it was one of my first, in fact) but was not able to get it published for nine years, after sending it out to almost every magazine I knew of.

"The Decline and Fall of Frankie Buller" could also be said to be autobiographical, but more for the life it portrays of young boys than for the authenticity of the main character. Frankie certainly existed though, and still does—a hale and forthright man who never did anyone any harm, and who, I am sure, never will. As for where it was written, the opening of the story speaks for itself.

Though I didn't realise it at the time of writing, "On Saturday Afternoon" was perhaps suggested by a few lines from the novel *The Eternal Husband* by Fyodor Dostoevsky which I had read some years before. In that novel it was a little girl who was watching a man about to hang himself, but in any case he was only pretending to do it so as to frighten her. At the time I had forgotten reading this, and did not remember it until recently. But my story of a little boy nonchalantly watching a despairing middle-aged man trying to commit suicide, is deadly serious and firmly embedded in its local setting. And who knows that the boy himself may not one day be in the same position as the unhappy man he is watching, since at the moment he seems to realise so little what it actually means? At the end of the story, however, one knows that such a thing will never be for him. What he is seeing is his own affirmation of life which, unfortunately, means another man's loss of it.

"The Fishing-boat Picture" was one of a pair owned by my parents, which I continually looked up at as a child. They were given to my mother and father as a wedding present but were sold (or pawned maybe) to get money for food at some time during the most indigent part of their married lives. This has nothing to do with the story, but is only to explain how the germ of it came about. The fishing-boat pictures were one of those crude cultural possessions that people are only too ready to trade for food or love should the necessity arise. The actual story, however, was "made up"—out of nothing.

So was "The Ragman's Daughter"—though my brother did once mention in a letter that a friend of his was going out with a girl who came to call for him on a horse. This picture must have worked in my mind for a year or so, until the embellishments fell into place, and I began to write it. It is hard to think of a good short story which is not at the same time tragic. Without tragedy there can be no art, a final sadness at the end which often makes us wonder why we are on earth at all if life at times can turn out to be so awful. Yet art must also contain those forceful seeds which state that since we *are* here we had better make the best of it for ourselves and for others.

Starting work at fourteen in a huge, all-embracing factory with its concomitants of overwhelming noise and totally mechanised society is a proud and yet stupifying moment in the life of any boy. The memory of this shock, which must subsequently have become traumatic though it did not seem so to me at the time, led me to write "The Bike". At least it formed the basis of it, wherein the physical shock of facing the onslaught of the factory on the senses was somewhat buffered by the moral shock of being sold a "hot" bike by a person who had appeared to be one's staunchest friend. I wrote the story in response to a letter from the literary editor of the *New Statesman*, who asked if I could provide one for the Christmas issue of 1960.

The final story in this collection is "The Firebug". It was built up piece by piece over several weeks, and I do not remember any idea or particular face coming to me that suggested the whole story. I believe I wrote the paragraph: "I smile as much as feel ashamed at the memory of some of the things I did when I was a lad, even though I caused my mother a lot of trouble. I used to pinch her matches and set fire to heaps of paper and anything I could get my eyes on". And I simply went on from there. The result is, I think, more of a study than a story, of a young boy whose precocious sexual awakening was perhaps sublimated by his desire to light fires on other people's property.

And so, finally, I think that a writer's first task (if some member of a poetry-reading audience insists that he have one at all) is to communicate with himself, and if he does this well enough, then he will make genuine contact with greater numbers than if he had erroneously tried to "communicate" with them more directly in the first place.

Torre Susaina
Deya
Majorca

For Comparison

One of the things we admire about many writers is the range and variety of the worlds that come to life in their words. Sillitoe's writing in this present collection hardly ventures outside the depressed Midlands industrial towns. In his other books (see pages 164–167) you will find a wider scope: the story of Brian Seaton in *Key to the Door*, for instance, reaches its climax in the Malayan jungle; Frank Dawes in *The Death of William Posters* finds his peace of mind after a gun-running episode in the Moroccan desert. And it is not merely a matter of settings. Sillitoe's characters are certainly not all drawn from the rebellious or stunted misfits of industrial cities.

Wider ranges, then, await the reader of Sillitoe's other books. From the point of view of *this* volume, though, the reader will also find echoes of some of the attitudes, ideas, and feelings of these stories in some of his other books. The brief anthology of extracts that follows picks up some of these themes as they appear in three of his other books, themes of the rebel against a society in which he has no legitimate place, the "honesty" of the rebel living by his own standards, the effects of cultural deprivation, and one picture of the depths of pointless and dejected effort to which poverty can force people.

Life Below the Poverty Line

(from *Key to the Door*)

Brian is growing up during the time of mass unemployed and gross poverty in the 1930s. As a young boy he joins the men who spend their days combing the Corporation rubbish-dumping ground for any scrap that might be saleable. Agger is one of the men; he has been there so long that he knows all the tricks of this way of raising a few shillings.

Eight-wheeled lorries came by the motorworks and followed each other towards the high flat tongue of land that had been raised by months of tipping and was slowly covering a non-descript area of reedgrass and water. From nearly every precipice men walked to where they hoped the loads would be dumped. Empty sacks flapped over their shoulders, and they called to each other, waving sticks and rakes. Brian, having already used his judgement, was scraping into a heap of swarf and scrap steel picked clean day's ago, but which still gave off a pleasant smell of aluminium shavings and carbolic, oil and the brass dust of big machines his father had sometimes worked. He kept one eye on the rapid movements of his flimsy rake, and the other on a small pile of wood covered with a sack nearby. Bert had promised to be at the tips later, and Brian hoped he'd come soon to get something from the four lorries—and the convoy of high-sided horsecarts trailing at walking pace behind.

"Where's it comin' from, mate?" Brian asked. Steelpins were popped out and the back ascended slowly. Half a dozen men, waiting for the avalanche of promise, watched the heavy handle being worked by a driver who rarely spoke to the scrapers, as if he were ashamed of being set within the luxurious world of hard labour. Even uncommitting banter was rare, and the scrapers looked on, waiting, never offering to help so as to get the stuff rolling sooner to their feet. "Prospect Street, young 'un," the driver answered.

Them old houses. A few bug-eaten laths. Wallpaper, dust and brick were already streaming down the bank, filling up oil-stained swamp-pools and crushing rusty tins at the bottom. A piece of wall made a splash like a bomb, and that was that. The back was wound up, and the lorry driven off. Brian rubbed pieces of cold water from his ear. Men were scraping systematically at the rammel, though expecting little from those poverty-stricken, condemned, fallen-down rabbit-holes on Prospect Street. Yet you never knew: such exercise in hope may gain a few brass curtain rings, a yard of decayed copperwire (from which the flex could be burned over the flames) or perhaps a piece of lead piping if it was a lucky day. A man whistled as he worked: speculation ran too high for speech.

Brian, having netted a few spars of wood, rubbed grit from his knees and stood up, gripped by a black, end-of-the-world hopelessness: Please, God, send a good tip, he said to himself. If you do I'll say Our Father. "What's up, kid?" Agger called from the top of the bank.

"I'm fed up," Brian said gloomily.

Men looked around, grinning or laughing. "Are yer 'ungry?" Brian said no, scraped a few half-bricks to reveal a fair-sized noggin of wood. "Sure? There's some bread and jam in my coat pocket if y'are," Agger said.

"No thanks. I've got some snap as well."

"What yer fed up for then?" He couldn't answer. Like the old man often said: Think yourself lucky you've got a crust o' bread in your fist. Then you can tek that sour look off your clock. But Brian couldn't. "What does your dad do?" Agger wanted to know.

"He's out o'work"—already forgetting despair.

Agger laughed. "He's got a lot o' company." Agger came on the tips every morning—in time for the first loads at nine—pushing an old carriage-pram, an antique enormous model that may once have housed some spoonfed Victorian baby and been pushed by a well-trimmed maid. There was no rubber on the wheels; all paint had long since blistered from its sides, and a makeshift piece of piping served for a handle. Another valued possession of Agger's was a real rake unearthed from a load of brick and tile tippings, an ornate brass-handled tool of the scraper's trade with which he always expected to pull up some treasure, good reaching under the muck for good, but which he used with relish whether it made him rich or not. Other scrapers envied it: Brian once heard one say: "Lend's your rake five minutes, Agger. I'll just get some wood for the fire." The men around stopped talking, and Agger stayed mute: just looked at the man—a faint touch of contempt at such ignorance of the rules of life—though the blank look was forced on to his face mainly because the request was unexpected, and unanswerable if he was to his sharp gispy-like dignity. The man got up and walked away, beyond the fire's warmth. "The daft bogger," Agger said loudly. "What does he tek me for? He wants chasing off the bleddy premises."

Agger often referred to the tips as 'the premises'—a high-flown name as if 'premises' was the one word and only loot he had carried off under his coat from some short term of employment—at being ordered off them himself by a despairing gaffer. 'Premises' to Agger was synonymous with some remote platform of life where order might have been created from the confusion within himself, if only he could be respected as king for some qualities he hadn't got—but wanted because he knew them to exist.

Winter and summer he wore a black overcoat that reached to his ankles and flapped around his sapling body. On the morning when his weekly gatherings had been sold to the scrapshop for a few shillings, each deep pocket of his coat held a quart bottle of tea, panniers that steadied the folds of an otherwise voluminous garment. Each morning he coaxed a fire from the abundant surface of the tip, stoked it to a beacon with old oil cloth, tar-paper and arms of brackenish wood that had laid between the floors and walls of back-to-back houses during generations both of people and bugs.

On fine days, Brian noticed, some scrapers worked little, stood talking by the fire, and only ran madly with coats waving when a lorry came; others scraped industriously every minute of the day whether there was a fresh tip or not, working solidified rubble on the off-chance of finding something that might have been missed. Brian belonged to the latter sort, searching the most unpromising loads because hope was a low-burning intoxication that never left him.

While the damp wind—seemingly foiled by jersey and coat—concentrated on Brian's face, he forgot it was also reaching into his body. He whistled a tune through a mixture of brick, wood-chippings and scraps of slate, feeling snatched only when the division between an unreal cotton-wool dreamland and the scratches on his numbed fingers broke down and flooded him with a larger sensation: 'snatched'—eyes and face muscles showing what the innermost body felt even though he hadn't been aware of it, perished through and through, so that a blazing fire would only bring smarting eyes and a skin thicker though not warmer.

Agger worked nearby, cleverly wrapped up and more impervious to cold because he had been on the tips longer than anyone else—straight from Flanders at twenty, he said. The useless slaughter of employable sinews had crashed his faith in guidance from men 'above' him, so that he preferred the tips even when there had been a choice. Sometimes he'd gaze into the quiet glass-like water of the nearby canal and sing to himself—a gay up-and-down tune without words—punctuating his Neanderthal quatrains with a handful of stones by aiming one with some viciousness into the water, watching the rings of its impact collide and disappear at the bank before breaking out again into another verse that came from some unexplored part of him. Born of a breaking-point, his loneliness was a brain-flashed at the boundary of his earthly stress. Still young looking, though lacking the jauntiness of youth, perhaps out of weakness he had seen the end too near the beginning, had grafted his body and soul into a long life on the tips even before his youth was finished. The impasse he lived in had compensations however, was the sort that made friends easily and even gave him a certain power over them.

Brian broke wood into small pieces and filled his sack, stuffing each bundle far down. "How are yer going to carry it?" Agger asked.

"On my back."

"It'll be too 'eavy."

"I'll drag it a bit then." After a pause for scraping, Agger wondered: "Do you sell it?"

"Sometimes."

"How much do you want for that lot?" Brian reckoned up: we've got plenty at home. I wain't mek much if I traipse it from door to door. "A tanner."

"I'll buy it," Agger said. "I know somebody as wants a

bit o' wood. I'll gi' yer the sack back tomorrow." Brian took the sixpence just as "Tip," someone screamed towards a corporation sewer-tank veering for the far side of the plateau. Agger ran quickly and Brian followed, more for sport since his only sackbag rested by Agger's pram.

He scrambled down the precipice to watch the back open above like a round oven door, a foul liquid stink pouring out. Then the body uptilted and a mass of black grate-and-sewer rubbish eased slowly towards the bank, coming out like an enormous sausage, quicker by the second, until it dropped all in a rush and splayed over the grass at the bottom. "Watch your boots," Agger shouted as he began scraping through it. "This stuff'll burn 'em off." He turned to Brian: "Don't come near this 'eap, nipper. You'll get fever and die if you do."

Brian stood back as half a lavatory bowl cartwheeled down from a lorry-load of house-rammel. "Tek a piss in that, Agger," the bowler shouted. It settled among petrol drums and Brian amused himself by throwing housebricks at it until both sides caved in. One of the men uncovered a length of army webbing: "Here's some o' your equipment from France, Agger"—throwing it like a snake at his feet.

Agger held it on the end of an inferior rake. "It ain't mine, mate. I chucked all my equipment in the water on my way back"— put his foot on it and continued scraping. The stench made Brian heave: he ran up the bank holding his nose, and stopped to breathe from fifty yards off.

Once a Rebel

(From *Saturday Night and Sunday Morning*)

Arthur Seaton, a young man of twenty-two, earns good money working on a lathe in a factory. Here are his thoughts as he works.

Once a rebel, always a rebel. You can't help being one. You can't deny that. And it's best to be rebel so as to show 'em it don't pay to try to do you down. Factories and labour exchanges and insurance offices keep us alive and kicking—so they say—but they're booby-traps and will suck you under like sinking-sands if you aren't careful. Factories sweat you to death, labour exchanges talk you to death, insurance and income tax offices milk money from your wage packets and rob you to death. And if you're still left with a tiny bit of life in your guts after all this boggering about, the army calls you up and you get shot to death. And if you're clever enough to stay out of the army you get bombed to death. Ay, by God, it's a hard life if you don't weaken, if you don't stop that bastard government from grinding your face in the muck, though there ain't much you can do about it unless you start making dynamite to blow their four-eyed clocks to bits.

They shout at you from soapboxes: "Vote for me, and this and that," but it amounts to the same in the end whatever you vote for because it means a government that puts stamps all over your phizzog until you can't see a hand before you, and what's more makes you buy 'em so's they can keep on doing it. They've got you by the guts, by backbone and skull, until they think you'll come whenever they whistle.

But listen, this lathe is my everlasting pal because it gets me thinking, and that's their big mistake because I know I'm not the only one. One day they'll bark and we won't run into a pen like sheep. One day they'll flash their lamps and clap their hands and say: "Come on, lads. Line-up and get your money. We won't let you starve." But maybe some of us will want to starve, and that'll be where the trouble'll start. Perhaps some'll want to play football, or go fishing up Grantham Cut. That big fat-bellied union ponce'll ask us not to muck things up. Sir Harold Bladdertab'll promise us a bigger bonus when things get put right. Chief Inspector Popcorn will say: "Let's have no trouble, no hanging around the gates there." Blokes with suits and bowler hats will say: "These chaps have got their television sets, enough to live on, council houses, beer and pools—some have even got cars. We've made them happy. What's wrong? Is that a machine-gun I hear starting up or a car backfiring?"

Der-der-der-der-der-der-der-der-der-der-der-der-der. I hope I'm not here to see it, but I know I will be. I'm a bloody billy-goat trying to screw the world, and no wonder I am, because it's trying to do the same to me.

The Honesty of a Rebel

(From *The Loneliness of the Long-Distance Runner*)

Smith, a Nottingham boy in Borstal for stealing, is running in the final of the inter-Borstal cross-country running cup. The Governor hopes he'll win the trophy for his Borstal. We learn Smith's thoughts as he runs; he reviews his past, considers the Governor's point of view, and sorts out his own mind.

I was in my element that afternoon knowing that nobody could beat me at running but intending to beat myself before the day was over. For when the governor talked to me of being honest when I first came in he didn't know what the word meant or he wouldn't have had me here in this race, trotting along in shimmy and shorts and sunshine. He'd have had me where I'd have had him if I'd been in his place: in a quarry breaking rocks until he broke his back. At least old Hitler-face the plain-clothes dick was honester than the governor, because he at any rate had had it in for me and I for him, and when my case was coming up in court a copper knocked at our front door at four o'clock in the morning and got my mother out of bed when she was paralytic tired, reminding her she had to be in court at dead on half past nine. It was the finest bit of spite I've ever heard of, but I would call it honest, the same as my mam's words were honest when she really told that copper what she thought of him and called him all the dirty names she'd ever heard of, which took her half an hour and woke the terrace up.

I trotted on along the edge of a field bordered by the sunken lane smelling green grass and honeysuckle, and I felt as though I came from a long line of whippets trained to run on two legs, only I couldn't see a toy rabbit in front and there wasn't a collier's cosh behind to make me keep up the pace. I passed the Gunthorpe runner whose shimmy was already black with sweat and I could just see the corner of the fenced-up copse in front where the only man I had to pass to win the race was going all out to gain the half-way mark. Then he turned into a tongue of trees and bushes where I couldn't see him anymore, and I couldn't see any-body, and I knew what the loneliness of the long-distance runner running across country felt like, realising that as far as I was concerned this feeling was the only honesty and realness there was in the world and I knowing it would be no different ever, no matter what I felt at odd times, and no matter what anybody else tried to tell me. The runner behind me must have been a long way off because it was so quiet, and there was even less noise and movement than there had been at five o'clock of a frosty winter morning. It was hard to understand, and all I knew was that you had to run, run, run, without knowing why you were running, but on you went through fields you didn't understand and into woods that made you afraid, over hills without knowing you'd been up and down, and shooting across streams that would have cut the heart out of you had you fallen into them. And the winning post was no end to it, even though crowds might be cheering you in, because on you had to go before you got your breath back, and the only time you stopped really was when you tripped over a tree trunk and broke your neck or fell into a disused well and stayed dead in the darkness forever. So I thought: they aren't going to get me on this racing lark, this running and trying to win, this jog-trotting for a bit of blue ribbon, because it's not the way to go on at all, though they swear blind that it is. You should think about nobody and go your own way, not on a course marked out for you by people holding mugs of water and bottles of iodine in case you fall and cut yourself so that they can pick you up—even if you want to stay where you are—and get you moving again.

On I went, out of the wood, passing the man leading without knowing I was going to do so. Flip-flap, flip-flap, jog-trot, jog-trot, crunchslap-crunchslap across the middle of a broad field again, rhythmically running in my greyhound effortless fashion, knowing I had won the race though it wasn't half over, won it if I wanted it, could go on for ten of fifteen or twenty miles if I had to and drop dead at the finish of it, which would be the same, in the end, as living an honest life like the governor wanted me to. It amounted to: win the race and be honest, and on trot-trotting I went, having the time of my life, loving my progress because it did me good and set me thinking which by now I liked to do, but not caring at all when I remembered that I had to win this race as well as run it. One of the two, I had to win the race or run it, and I knew I could do both because my legs had carried me well in front—now coming to the short cut down the bramble bank and over the sunken road— and would carry me further because they seemed made of electric cable and easily alive to keep on slapping at those ruts and roots, but I'm not going to win because the only way I'd see I came in first would be if winning meant that I was going to escape the coppers after doing the biggest bank job of my life, but winning means the exact opposite, no matter how they try to kill or kid me, means running right into their white-gloved wall-barred hands and grinning mugs and staying there for the rest of my natural long life of stone-breaking anyway, but stone-breaking in the way I want to do it and not in the way they tell me.

Another honest thought that comes is that I could swing left at the next hedge of the field, and under its cover beat my slow retreat away from the sports ground winning post. I could do three or six or a dozen miles across the turf like this and cut a few main roads behind me so's they'd never know which one I'd taken; and maybe on the last one when it got dark I could thumb a lorry-lift and get a free ride north with somebody who might not give me away. But no, I said I wasn't daft didn't I? I won't pull out with only six months left, and besides there's nothing I want to dodge and run away from; I only want a bit of my own back on the In-laws and Potbellies by letting them sit up there on their big posh seats and watch me lose this race, though as sure as God made me I know that when I do lose I'll get the dirtiest crap and kitchen jobs in the months to go before my time is up. I won't be worth a threpp'ny-bit to anybody here, which will be all the thanks I get for being honest in the only way I know. For when the governor told me to be honest it was meant to be in his way not mine, and if I kept on being honest in the way he wanted and won my race for him he'd see I got the cushiest six months still left to run; but in my own way, well, it's not allowed, and if I find a way of doing it such as I've got now then I'll get what-for in every mean trick he can set his mind to. And if you look at it in my way, who can blame him? For this is war—and ain't I said so?—and when I hit him in the only place he knows he'll be sure to get his own back on me for not collaring that cup when his heart's been set for ages on seeing himeself standing up at the end of the afternoon to clap me on the back as I take the cup from Lord Earwig or some such chinless wonder with a name like that. And so I'll hit him where it hurts a lot, and he'll do all he can to get his own back, tit for tat, though I'll enjoy it most because I'm hitting first, and because I planned it longer. I don't know why I think these thoughts are better than any I've ever had, but I do, and I don't care why. I suppose it took me a long time to get going on all this because I've had no time and peace in all my bandit life, and now my thoughts are coming pat and the only trouble is I often can't stop, even when my brain feels as if it's got cramp, frostbite and creeping paralysis all rolled into one and I have to give it a rest by slap-dashing down through the brambles of the sunken lane. And all this is another upper-cut I'm getting in first at people like the governor, to show how—if I can—his races are never won even though some bloke always comes unknowingly in first, how in the end the governor is going to be doomed while blokes like me will take the pickings of this roasted bones and dance like maniacs around his Borstal's ruins. And so this story's like the race and once again I won't bring off a winner to suit the governor; no, I'm being honest like he told me to, without him knowing what he means, though I don't suppose he'll ever come in with a story of his own, even if he reads this one of mine and knows who I'm talking about.

Escape into Books

(From *Key to the Door*)

Brian's parents are very poor, his father on the dole. Brian has become fascinated with the thought of owning a book of his own, and has saved up for weeks to buy a 2s 6d book. Knowing that it would be very difficult to save the money at home, he paid sixpence at a time to the shop. In this excerpt he brings home the book which he has at last paid for.

True to his promise, Dave donated the final threepence. Saturday afternoon was warm and dusty, and he walked to Canning Circus, past old houses being knocked down, lorries lining-up to transport rammel to the Sann-eye tips. Crossing the complicated junction he descended via Derby Road, looking into each shop, wondering as he skirted Slap Square what his mother and father would say when they saw him come into the house holding a thick and fabulous book.

A large atlas was opened at a map of the world, surrounded by dictionaries and foreign language books—the only section of the shop that interested him. He went in, and told a brown-dressed girl by the cash-desk that he wanted to buy *The Count of Monte-Cristo*, started to explain the simple financial system into which he had entered.

She left him standing with four pink receipts and the final sixpence, and came back with the manager. "I know him," he said. "He's a customer of ours." He turned to Brian, took the receipts and money and spread them on the cash-desk. "*The Count of Monte-Cristo* wasn't it? Go and get it for him, will you?"

The book came, and he had only time to glimpse the picture-cover of a man holding a sword before it was taken away and wrapped up.

He opened the packet outside, flipped the hundreds of pages through his fingers, from cover to cover and back again. A posh woman's voice said from behind: "You're going to be busy, aren't you?" He turned and said yes, ran his eyes up and down the formidable list of chapter titles.

No one was at home, and he sat by the fire to read. The room had been scrubbed and the table cleared, and in the congenial emptiness he sped on through the easy prose of the story, had reached Edmond Dantès' betrothal ceremony before his parents came in. They took off their coats. "That looks a nice book," his mother said. "Where did you get it from?"

"I bought it from downtown."

"Who gen you all *that* money?" his father put in.

"It must 'ave cost a pretty penny," his mother said, spreading the cloth for tea.

"Nobody gen me the money," Brian told them, closing the book carefully. "I saved it up."

Irritation came into his mother's voice: "How much was it?"

"Half a crown."

"Yer've wasted 'alf a crown on a book?" His father exclaimed.

He'd imagined they'd be pleased at his cleverness in bringing such a thing into the house, but it was the opposite. It was as though he'd been split in half and was bleeding to death. All for a book. "It was *my* money," he cried, anguished and bitter, because instead of buying the book he should have given the money to them.

"You're bloody-well silly about books," his father said, a definite threat in this voice. "You read till you're bloody-well daft." His mother came back from the kitchen: "You stand need to spend half a crown on books when you ain't got a bit o' shoe to your feet. And you're a sly little swine to 'ave money in the 'ouse all that time when I've often bin wi'out a shillin' ter buy some snap."

"I didn't have the money here," he explained. "I took it bit by bit to the bookshop, like a Christmas club." This was even worse, because he'd made sure that, starving or not, they hadn't been able to get their hands on it.

"You'd 'ave 'ad more sense to a got yoursen a pair o' shoes," Seaton cried. "I've a good mind to throw it on the bleddy fire."

"'E's got no more sense than 'e was born with," his

mother said. Brian was horrified at his father's threat, saw flames already at their work. "It's *my* book," he shouted.

"Don't cheek me," Seaton said, "or you'll be for it, my lad." His tears were open, and they saw it. "I hope there's a war on soon so's we're all killed," he raved.

"What a thing to say," his mother said. "I don't know where he gets it from."

A smack across the head from his father. "Say one more word, and I'll show yer what I'll do wi' yer."

"Wait till I grow up," Brain cried.

But Seaton only said: "He'll be a lunatic one day wi' reading so many books."

He sat by the fire while they drank tea, trying to force back the sobs, difficult because he saw too easily how he had done wrong. But hatred and pity for himself surmounted this, and so he couldn't stop. Vera passed him some tea: "Come on, it ain't end o' the world." His eyes were drawn to the book cover, where a brave man held a rapier as if he didn't care for anyone in the world, as though nothing could ever trouble him. And if it did, the face and sword said, it would be an easy matter to fight a duel and dispose of whatever it was.

He ate bread and jam, and went on reading. The story grafted itself to him, slowly becoming him and he becoming it, and he left behind with each second the light and noise in the house and went on wondering footsteps down into the dungeons of the Château d'If with Edmond Dantès, following the guards and slipping invisibly into the cell, and all night long he listened to the tapping and whispers that came from the granite floor, heard the patient scraping and scratching of freedom, was shown that even dungeons and giant prisons were unable to keep men in forever, though fourteen years was longer by four than he had so far lived: he listened to the chipping of home-made tools, and voices whispering as if from the dead, that talked of knowledge and freedom and hidden treasure on the Island of Monte-Cristo.

Thinking over the Stories

Some readers may be depressed by these stories; others even disgusted by the sordid crime and squalor. Most will surely be moved to feel for the characters, and to think about their plight. Few readers could come away from the stories without some interlocking of their minds with the feelings and ways of Sillitoe's people. Even fewer could, I think, ever completely forget some of the scenes: Uncle Ernest, for instance returning to the oblivion of the pub, or Frankie Buller setting off through the traffic to a cowboy film.

The stories are memorable, and so they are worth thinking over. Having read them once, we may be able to increase our understanding and deepen our enjoyment by considering some points about the way in which they are written.

Telling the Story

All but two of these stories are written as if in the very words of a real story-teller. The reader is button-holed, as it were, by the first remark, often casually slipped out but designed to hold the listener's attention:

> The Easter I was fifteen I sat at the table for supper and Mam said to me: "I'm glad you've left school. Now you can go to work."

Perhaps this fondness for the story-teller has come from the author's idea of the "ideal story":

> . . . a narrative spoken aloud by an illiterate man to a group surrounding a fire in the forest at night, or told by a man to his friends in a pub, or at the table during dinner-hour in a canteen.

When you think back over these story-tellers, you realise that the author has found for each a different way of speaking, a different frame of mind and idiom of language. Some of the differences are easy to hear:

> Sitting in what has come to be called my study, a room in the first-floor flat of a ramshackle Majorcan house, my eyes move over racks of books around me. Row after row of coloured backs and dusty tops, they give an air of distinction not only to the room, but to the whole flat, and one can sense the thoughts of occasional visitors who stoop down discreetly during drinks to read their titles.

> I've never known a family to look as black as our family when they're fed-up. I've seen the old man with his face so dark and full of murder because he ain't got no fags or was having to use saccharine to sweeten his tea, or even for nothing, that I've backed out of the house in case he got up from his fireside chair and came for me. He just sits, almost on top of the fire, his oil-stained Sunday-joint maulers opened out in front of him and facing inwards to each other, his thick shoulders scrunched forward, and his dark brown eyes staring into the fire.

The difference here is not just in the scene being described; it is also in the *way* of speaking. Thc vocabulary suits the invented character of the speaker: "stoop down discreetly", says the first; "scunched forward", the second. More than that, the tone differs. The first is sophisticated and self-conscious ("an air of distinction") with a somewhat deliberate sentence rhythm; the second is blurted out, with rambling sentences. These differences and the reasons for them are obvious. The close reader, though, will sense differences even between characters as seemingly similar as Tony in "The Ragman's Daughter" and Colin in "The Bike."

The story-telling voice, then, is suited to the supposed teller. But it is worth noting that the way of speaking is not necessarily completely "realistic". This is not "tape-recorder" dialogue. Whatever the character, he tells his tale with style and a dramatic sense of timing. Look at this snippet from "The Bike":

> A copper came, and the man was soon flicking out his wallet, showing a bill with the number of the bike on it: proof right enough. But I still thought he'd made a mistake. "You can tell us all about that at the Guildhall," the copper said to me.

This is an economical account of the incident; it is in character, that is it has the ring of Colin to it, but it is also *effective* story-telling in its own right, concentrating on the key details, punching out the key phrases. This quality becomes very clear if you read these stories aloud to an audience. The stories spring to life, and almost act themselves out.

The apparent casualness of the story-telling should not make the close reader overlook a final point about the use of a narrator: we learn much about the tale from the asides, shifts of meaning, and changes of mind of the teller:

> "What's up, mam?" I said—or whined I expect, because I could only whine up to fourteen: then I went to work and started talking clear and proper, from shock.

> I've been a postman for twenty-eight years. Take that first sentence: because it's written in a simple way may make the fact of my having been a postman for so long seem important, but I realise that such a fact has no significance whatever. After all, it's not my fault that it may seem as if it has to some people just because I wrote it down plain; I wouldn't know how to do it any other way. If I started using long and complicated words that I'd searched for in the dictionary I'd use them too many times, the same ones over and over again, with only a few sentences—if that—between each one; so I'd rather not make what I'm going to write look foolish by using dictionary words.

You will notice also that we get interesting comparisons between the story-teller at the time of his telling ("now", as it were), and his old remembered self. These comparisons help us to 'place' the incidents and to see the characters fully and in the round.

The Shape of the Stories

We don't find in these stories trick endings or apparent and obvious patterning or shaping of the story. They often seem to slip out casually, the only structure being just the result of the spurts and lapses of the story-teller's memory. Look at "The Bike," for instance. We slide into it rapidly; within a few words we know where we are and what's what. We are given two carefully pared-down snatches of conversation, with a tiny but important fragment of Colin's private thoughts sandwiched in between. ("That's the trouble with me: I'm not clever."), and the next stage of the story has started:

> Going to the bike factory to ask for a job meant getting up early, just as if I was back at school; there didn't seem any point in getting older.

In a close reading you'll find the story is instinctively and surely "built up". You can almost *feel* the relationship between the teller and his audience, as he lets the tension slacken, suddenly pulls the story together to a sharp climax, and then effortlessly slips away on some sideline. For instance, later in the story the bike sale is clinched and the story has reached a small climax. Before Colin can tell us of the actual handing over of the bike the next morning, we have a contrasting scene with his Dad at home. Notice the effect of the small and apparently unconnected story about his father which he slips in:

> Dad was already in when I got home, filling the kettle at the scullery tap. I don't think he felt safe without there was a kettle on the gas. "What would you do if the world suddenly ended, Dad?" I once asked when he was in a good mood "Mash some tea and watch it," he said. He poured me a cup.
> "Lend's five bob, Dad, till Friday." . . .

This is skilful art: the suspense is increased by a pause and a moment of relaxation.

Sillitoe gives us a clue to his aim and method on page 128:

> I see such a story not as an incident which begins at point A and goes in a line thinly but straight to point B, but rather as a circuitous embellishment, twisting and convoluted, meandering all over the place until, near the end, these irrelevencies can at last be seen to have a point, and so can now come together on the main theme and climax.

To achieve this "circuitous embellishment . . . meandering all over the place" careful, not casual, writing is required, particularly if all is to "be seen to have a point" and if the whole piece is to "come together on the main theme and climax". Look for instance at "Noah's Ark": it has no real "story", and may be felt to be very bittily and casually made up, but it all "slots in". Look at the last sentence: the rowdy noise of the boys' singing dies away in the night air, but Colin tries to keep the sound of the singing in his mind to drive away the memory of the fair:

> But to Colin, the noise stayed, all around their heads and faces, grinding away the sight and sound of the Noah's Ark jungle he had ridden on free, and so been pitched from.

He had escaped his conscience and spent, on the dreamland of the fair, the pennies that could (and should) have gone to his family. In a desperate attempt to make the dreamland last longer, Colin had also cheated, but reality had harshly caught up with him and "so" he was thrown off the Noah's Ark. The story ends, then, with its central point, one which it picks up from the second page:

> The thought of what fourpence would do to the table at home filled him—when neither spoke—with spasms of deep misery.

Another example of the narrative skill is the close weaving in and out of the present with flashbacks. This is a method

Sillitoe uses in his full-length novels; *Key to the Door*, for instance, contrasts Brian Seaton's experiences in Malaya with his earlier life in Nottingham. "The Loneliness of the Long-Distance Runner" weaves into the description of the final race Smith's memories of his criminal career. In our collection there is something of this mixing and mingling in most of the stories, most fully in "The Ragman's Daughter".

A Sense of Place

The words of the well-established author Robert Graves to the young Sillitoe in Majorca are important (see page 162). He advised him to write about Nottingham, "the town I grew up in and which I still seemed attached to judging by my colourful remarks about it in conversation". To most readers this is an unattractive townscape:

> The overhead lights made us look TB.

> The noise of the turnery hit me like a boxing glove as I went in.

> Outside the air wasn't so fresh, what with that bloody great bike factory bashing away at the yard-end.

> Mildewed backyards and houses full of silverfish and black-clocks when you suddenly switch on the light at night.

But Sillitoe's writing reveals also a certain affection for the town: its streets, yards, canal, pubs, traffic, and grime. The Goose Fair can give the ordinary streets a glamour:

> Along each misty street they went, aware at every turning of a low exciting noise from the northern sky. Bellies of cloud were lighted orange by the fair's reflection.

But even the everyday street can be felt to have a certain splendour. Despite its emphasis on the dirt, this passage from "Uncle Ernest" is not lacking in affection:

> Chimes to the value of half past ten boomed from the Council-house clock. Over the theatre patches of blue

> sky held hard-won positions against autumnal clouds, and a treacherous wind lashed out its gusts, sending paper and cigarette packets cartwheeling along unswept gutters.

There is some delight to be found in the town by the author, who knows it so intimately, but it is a delight that comes and goes, and is frequently replaced by dejection. Many of the characters in Sillitoe's stories dream of distant towns or foreign countries as an excape for the town that hems them in. Others escape physically, and many of the moments of pleasure in the stories take place outside the town, for "the fields weren't all that far from the black and smothercating streets". (A telling word that "smothercating".)

To a reader living in a town like London, with its sprawling suburbs, it may be difficult to realise how close the country is to the densely packed streets of Nottingham: the boy in "The Firebug" sets off from his yard and is in a wood not long after. Colin buys his bike for this escape; Tony takes Doris to it; and, to give an example from another book, Arthur escapes to it in *Saturday night and Sunday Morning*. Here he is fishing, and the fighting selfishness that is his main characteristic in the town seems softer in these surroundings:

> He sat by the canal fishing on a Sunday morning in spring, at an elbow where alders dipped over the water like old men on their last legs, pushed by young sturdy oaks from behind. He straightened his back, his fingers freeing nylon line from a speedily revolving reel. Around him lay knap-sack and jacket, an empty catch-net, his bicycle, and two tins of worms dug from the plot of garden at home before setting out. Sun was breaking through clouds, releasing a smell of earth to heaven. Birds sang. A soundless and miniscular explosion of water caught his eye. He moved nearer the edge, stood up, and with a vigorous sweep of his arm, cast out the line.
>
> Another solitary man was fishing further along the canal, but Arthur knew thay they would leave each other in peace, would not even call out greetings. No one

bothered you: you were a hunter, a dreamer, your own boss, away from it all for a few hours on any day that the weather did not throw down its rain. Like the corporal in the army who said it was marvellous the things you thought about as you sat on the lavatory. Even better than that, it was marvellous the things that came to you in the tranquillity of fishing.

Whether they are attractive or depressing, the places in Sillitoe's stories are brought vividly to our senses: the Goose Fair in "Noah's Ark"; the sitting-room in "Fishing-boat Picture"; the café in "Uncle Ernest"; the factory in "The Bike". All the stories, in fact, have a strong sense of place so that the surroundings are often almost a character in the story.

A Working-Class Writer?

Because Alan Sillitoe had little formal education and because his first two books had working-class characters and settings he was given by some the label "Working-Class Author". Sillitoe said of *Saturday Night and Sunday Morning*: "The greatest inaccuracy was ever to call the book a 'working-class novel' for it is really nothing of the sort. It is simply a novel." This is equally true of these stories: they are simply about *people* in a particular social class, not about *examples* of a particular sort of person.

Yet it is true that Sillitoe describes provincial working-class backgrounds better and more fully than most writers before him. To that extent the label was probably inevitable. But his real achievement was to write about these environments without self-consciousness. He is not decking out his characters with a colourful background setting, but simply bringing their ways of life to the printed page. Perhaps the label has got some use, then, if it helps us to see that whereas other writers have "used" or "brought in" working-class background, Sillitoe simply writes about it, both more accurately and less sentimentally. Compare these two brief extracts, for instance. They both refer to the effects of poverty on a family in the 1930s. One makes the picture charming and rather "touching"; the other gloomy and lifeless. One is from a very popular book with a "working-class setting"; the other is from one of Sillitoe's books. Which is the "working-class author" writing from firsthand, and which the "middle-class author" looking from a distance?

> A great deal was heard about boots in the Ruggles household. They were always wearing out and being taken to the little shop round the corner to be "soled and heeled", and "tipped" with bits of iron or rubber in order to try and make them last a little longer. Nearly every week one of the little Ruggles could be seen running with a boot in either hand to the shop, or returning with a bulky parcel badly wrapped in old brown paper.

> One Thursday afternoon Vera said: "Go up Ilkeston Road, Brian, and meet your dad. He'll be on his way back from the dole-office. Tell 'im to get five Woodbines and bring 'alf a pound of fish for our suppers. Go on, run, he'll gi' you ha'penny if you see him." Brian gathered what brother was available, and did as he was told.
>
> Vera had been glad to see the back of her husband that morning. Hunched by the fireplace, sulking because he had no cigarettes and was out of work at thirty-five, he suddenly stood up and took his dole-cards from the cupboard. "I'll have a walk," was his way of putting it, "and call in at the dole-office on my way back."

The Ideas and Attitudes

It is an easy trap to fall into when reading fiction to take the voice of one of the characters as the voice of the author, speaking directly to the reader. This is doubly easy when the story is written as if spoken by an "I" that could be the author himself reminiscing. If you know, as we do, that the stories have a setting similar to that of the author's own early life, the trap is even harder to avoid.

It is important, therefore, to be quite clear that these stories are *fiction*, the remarks are not necessarily the author's own views, and (even in "Frankie Buller" where the story-teller is a writer called Alan) we cannot take any of the characters to be a straight autobiographical picture of the author. We must therefore be careful not to label as "Alan Sillitoe's" ideas and attitudes which he has created for his characters.

Still, there are some themes or ideas behind the stories which keep appearing in these and others of Sillitoe's early writings. The "Questions for Writing or Discussion" later on may help readers to think about the point behind individual stories. Here it is worth looking more generally at some of the writer's concerns and preoccupations.

First, perhaps, one is struck by Sillitoe's understanding of the forces that drive some people to rebel against society. *Saturday Night and Sunday Morning* and "The Loneliness of the Long-Distance Runner" are explorations of different kinds of rebels, and the extracts on pages 139 and 141 show the way the characters' minds work. You can compare these with the words of the boy in "On Saturday Afternoon", Colin in "The Bike", Tony in "The Ragman's Daughter", and even Alan in the last story, when he comments on the medical approach to Frankie. In all these characters there is a strong feeling of a wide split between "them" in authority over "us", whose only hope of a free life is to rebel and to enjoy rebellion. It is a rebellion conditioned by, so to speak, the tribal memory of poverty, but not necessarily directly influenced by the most pressing needs of poverty now. As the worst material effects of poverty were somewhat improved with the growth of the welfare state after the Second World War, the nation thought that much of the pre-war crime, violence, and class resentment would disappear. It didn't, and around the time Sillitoe's first novel was published (1958) the "respectable" public were baffled and resentful. "Why", they asked loudly, "are people still kicking against the community when so much is being done for them?" Of course, there is no simple answer, but Alan Sillitoe is able to sympathise with these rebels to a considerable extent, and so we as readers also for a while look at the world with the point of view of a person who is "agin" it all.

For a reader who wants to think more about this aspect of the stories, there are various books of facts and arguments about society. Specially recommended is Chapter 3 of *The Uses of Literacy* by Richard Hoggart (Chatto and Windus, or Penguin Books). Richard Hoggart tries to describe working-class life in England, and the changes that modern society, and particularly the modern entertainments of newspapers, magazines, television, is making. The book was first published the year before Sillitoe's first novel, and you will see from this quotation that in factual sociological terms it touches on something of the same idea:

> "They" are "the people at the top", "the higher-ups", the people who give you your dole, call you up, tell you to go to war, fine you, made you split the family in the thirties to avoid a reduction in the Means Test allowance, "get yer in the end", "aren't to be trusted really", "talk posh", "are all twisters really", "never tell yer owt" (e.g. about a relative in hospital), "clap yer in clink", "will do y'down if they can", "summons yer", "are all in a click (clique) together", "treat y' like muck".

This gathering together of *typical* attitudes can be compared with Arthur Seaton's outburst on page 139.

Connected in some ways with this understanding of rebelliousness is Sillitoe's frequent reference to the poverty of many of the characters' lives, not in money but in family life and, particularly, opportunities to enjoy a range of entertainments, especially books. He refers to this in his introduction when he is speaking about "Noah's ark." (page 129). The extract on page 145 from *Key to the Door* makes it clear how enriching the world of books and the imaginative extension of literature can be to the young child, particularly perhaps the poor child. All the young people in these stories are affected to some extent or other by what the sociologists call "cultural deprivation"—they just haven't got a great deal to do and, despite ingenuity and a warm family life in a few cases, their lives are very limited. Think of the boy, for instance, in "The Firebug":

> The long school holidays of summer seemed to go on for years. When I could scrounge fourpence I'd nip to the continuous downtown pictures after dinner and drop

myself in one of the front seats, to see the same film over and over till driven out by hunger or God save the King . . . .

Sillitoe is particularly good at seeing the child's point of view; he does not look down at the child, but looks at the world from the child's height. We see often the dawning consciousness of the adult world on a child. This is a focus which allows the reader a fresh, in some ways uncomplicated, scrutiny of life. For instance, in "On Saturday Afternoon" the attempted suicide is stripped of all the complications which an adult would see in it. The boy does ask "What are yer going to do it for, mate?", but he has no close interest in the complications of the motive. To him the man is "feeling black", an acute case but a case of something which he himself feels sometimes, and his father often. The story is in fact about the boy, not the man, and its climax is not the unsuccessful suicide or the later successful attempt, but the boy's dawning understanding that there are different levels of being "fed up".

It is a pointless task to try to explain what makes an author choose to weave his words round one incident and group of characters and not another, but if one tried to say what ideas or attitudes these stories had in common the answer might be something like the description Sillitoe himself gave of his book *The General*: "The two sides of the question of civilisation versus barbarism." In that book the "good things" of life are represented by art and the "bad things" by "military warfare". In these stories barbarism is seen to be embodied in deadness and lack of feeling, and civilisation by a liveliness and an ability to feel and relish despite apalling dreariness of surroundings.

Enjoying the Stories

The danger in writing about fiction in this way is that it easily can seem to be a matter of "devices" and "skills". When one thinks over these stories, though, one might remember Sillitoe's own description of ideal story-telling, to be told "with patience and understanding and love" (*page* 129). These stories are well written certainly, but their quality is best described in those three words, and perhaps in Sillitoe's description of good writing: "the final matching of truth and language". The truth we experience in these stories (and it is important that we *experience* it and are not merely told of it) is the understanding of people, what outside factors and what inner compulsion make them as they are. Some of these people are likeable (Colin); some have no scruples (Tony); others are pathetic (Ernest); and one seems to be almost dead to feeling (Harry). In each case their essential humanity is brought home to use not by a sentimental glossing over of their failings, but by the author's shrewd compassion.

The Author and his Books

Alan Sillitoe was born in Nottingham in 1928. He went to various elementary schools until he was fourteen, when he started work in the Raleigh Bicycle factory at Coventry, where his father also worked. As a boy he used to tell stories to his brothers and sisters, and he even did a little writing of what he calls "doggerel verse and a few essays" when he was twelve and thirteen, but he had no interest in literature; he says himself: "until I was nineteen, I didn't think of writing at all. I was just having a good time like any other young man; I was working in a factory and spending my money".

At eighteen he was called up and joined the R.A.F., spending nearly two years in Malaya as a wireless operator. It was during this time that he started reading. He left the Air Force with tuberculosis, and had to spend eighteen months in hospital. He has described this time in his introduction to *Saturday Night and Sunday Morning* in the Heritage of Literature Series:

> Before then I had hardly read any 'adult' books, but during my enforced retirement from life, and to absorb the shock of it, I read hundreds. In that short time I caught up with most other young people who had gone through grammar school and on to university. In the next few years I may even have surpassed them in the range of my reading.
>
> During this time I also began to write, mostly poems, but one or two short stories. At twenty-one I wrote my first novel. In seventeen days I wrote the whole hundred thousand words of it. It was some years before I was able to see how bad it was, illiterate in fact, ungrammatical, and derivative of Lawrence, Huxley, and Dostoyevsky, and of anyone else whose books I may have been reading

at the time. It was, in other words, a failure, as were the half dozen other novels written before *Saturday Night and Sunday Morning* began to take shape under the orange trees of Majorca, a few miles from where I am writing now.

My apprenticeship took ten years—from writing my first juvenile poems to getting this novel published, from the age of twenty to the age of thirty. So now I have been "published" for as long as it took me to learn to write, and also in that time ten books of mine have been printed.

I was learning to read while I was learning to write, becoming familiar with the best authors and the great novels of the world. It is impossible to say which novels influenced me most, though not difficult to tell which I most enjoyed reading. *The Good Soldier Schweik, Nostromo, Tom Jones, Wuthering Heights, The Charterhouse of Parma*—I remember them easily because each one I read more than once. No person advised me to, or told me what they meant or what to look for in them, but from the first pages I knew there was a magic spirit, a delight in these books that was easy to see, indestructable and unforgettable. I read some pages of each aloud, and gradually, through writing so much of my own, began to see what could be made of language, how with skill, patience, hard work, and having something to say, I could write stories and novels of my own.

After leaving hospital Alan Sillitoe was given a small pension. He went abroad, and managed to spin this out for a number of years, supplementing it by giving English lessons, doing translations, and working for tourist agencies. He was writing all the time, getting nothing published and destroying a great deal. He wrote a number of short stories and incidents about a young man in Nottingham, but most of his writing seems to have been based on "fantasies" rather than his own experiences. He says:

I was living in Majorca at the time, and had become friendly with Robert Graves. I showed him a novel of mine already written, some fantasy creation which had no basis in reality and little in fact. He suggested that what I really ought to do was write something—a novel perhaps—which was set in Nottingham, the town I had grown up in and which I still seemed attached to judging by my colourful remarks about it in conversation.

A year later Sillitoe gathered together his "Nottingham" pieces, and in about eighteen months wrote his first published novel, *Saturday Night and Sunday Morning*. This was received with great praise, winning a prize for the best novel of 1958, and it was soon made into a successful film.

As we have seen on page 156, it would be very inaccurate to think of Sillitoe as a "purely autobiographical" writer. Yet it is probably the Nottingham working-class life and the pressure of the experiences as a child of the 1930s depression that gave him his most powerful urge to write. It is interesting for readers still at school to wonder about the effects of leaving school so early. Sillitoe himself has spoken about one of the disadvantages in a radio interview after the publication of his third book:

I found it very difficult to write good English. I feel that many writers have a certain advantage if they went to a University. . . . These early writings were so naïve; you'd use the same word about ten times on one page, a word you'd discovered the day before, and so on, and it took me a long time to throw off these habits and get to know how to write.

One might have thought that lacking lengthy formal education he would have found it easy to "be himself", and yet he couldn't. He confesses his difficulties:

A big question I often ask myself is why I didn't write *Saturday Night and Sunday Morning* when I was twenty-two say, or twenty-three, but I couldn't do this because all the earlier novels were mostly about fantasies or they were pastiches of other writers, like Lawrence and Dostoyevsky; they were, shall we say, in a middle-class world, and it took me a long time to get out of that and begin to feel my own feet, and know that what I should write about was the life I knew in Nottingham which was the most vivid to me.

"To feel my own feet"—this was the problem. To have the confidence to write about what he knew well and felt deeply was difficult, and to find the language in which to create his stories was equally difficult. It was as if he had to struggle through a false period of trying other people's modes and self-consciously enriching his language before he could develop a theme and a way of writing firmly his own.

Readers who have enjoyed these stories will probably like to find other books by the author. Here are notes on those which are most likely to be enjoyed by student readers, and then a list of all his books. (Educational editions are given when they are available.)

Saturday Night and Sunday Morning

(Longmans' Heritage of Literature Series, with an introduction by the author)
Sillitoe's own description of the book is: "It is a novel mainly about one man, a twenty-two year old factory worker in Nottingham, and covers two years of his life." The chief character, Arthur Seaton, finds only the slightest satisfaction in his job at a lathe in a factory; he feels he owes society nothing, and for him life is drink and women in the evenings.

The Loneliness of the Long-distance Runner

(Longmans' Heritage of Literature Series)
This is a long tale (nearly twice as long as the longest in this book) about a rebellious Nottingham youth in Borstal for theft. There he is specially favoured by the Governor who, proud of the sporting reputation of his Borstal, hopes that the youth will win the inter-Borstal cross-country trophy. We see the Governor's phoney qualities and the emptiness of the accepted social standards through the mind of the youth whose experience of life so far, particularly his family and the death of his father, has given him a feeling for his own

"honesty". The boy enjoys running and the feeling of freedom it gives him, but he feels he is being used by the Governor merely to get the cup. His dramatic gesture is deliberately to lose the big race at the final stage in front of the "pot bellied pop eyes" and "goldfish mouths" of the visitors. This he feels to be more "honest" in his sense of the word than is the behaviour of the Governor.

Key to the Door (W. H. Allen)

This was the fifth of Sillitoe's books to be published, though only the third novel. It is a very long book that could almost be called "the story of a generation". We see a man's first twenty-one years through the eyes of Brian Seaton, a Nottingham boy: growing up in pre-war days, his early manhood, work, and marriage, and his time as a conscript National Serviceman in the R.A.F. in Malaya. The climax to the book is a hand-to-hand fight with a Chinese communist in the jungle. Brian's behaviour and feelings at this point are the result, we realise, of all the earlier incidents.

A Complete List

(The date of first publication is given. The general edition is published by W. H. Allen unless otherwise stated.)

Saturday Night and Sunday Morning (1958)

The Loneliness of the Long-Distance Runner (1959)

As well as the title story, this contains eight other stories, five of which are in this selection.

The General (1960)

Unlike Sillitoe's other books, this is set in the future, during an imaginary east-west war, in which a symphony orchestra, sent to entertain troops, is captured by the other side. The General, whose men have captured the orchestra, has been instructed to kill all prisoners. However, he is a music-lover, and orders that they should give a performance, and eventually he helps them to escape. For this he is disgraced, though his career is not quite broken; but he feels he has done right. Sillitoe himself has pointed out that this is related to his other books and indeed his own background. He has stressed that "if you take in this book *The General* the two sides of the question of civilisation versus barbarism, or the good things of life represented by art and the bad things by military warfare and so on, that situation exists or did exist in my own brain before I became a writer".

The Rats and Other Poems (1960)

Sillitoe had been writing some poetry at the same time as his early novels. This collection has a number of short pieces and one long poem, which he describes as an attack on "the old notions of war, patriotism and national insularity".

The Ragman's Daughter (1963)

This was Sillitoe's second volume of stories; it includes the title story and two others from this selection.

Road to Volgograd (1964)

A vivid account of a month's visit to Russia.

A Falling Out of Love and Other Poems (1964)

The Death of William Posters (1965)

The central character, Frank Dawley, is a thoughtful working man who feels himself "taken over", so to speak, by his other self, whom he calls William Posters, a man killed by the lack of humanity in his job, his routine of life, and the whole of industrialism. Dawley leaves his job, his wife, and his home, and sets off in search of something fresh. Eventually he feels the old William Posters is dead.

Citizens are Soldiers (1967)

This is an unpublished play, originally commissioned by the National Theatre, but not staged by them. It was first performed in 1967. The text is built round a translation of a seventeenth century Spanish playright, Lope da Vega. The original play shows how all members of a village band together to protect themselves against the oppression of the local commanders.

Tree of Fire (1967) Macmillans

Questions for Writing or Discussion

The Bike

1 Has Colin thought much about work so far? What does he expect from 'a job'?

2 What are his first impressions of the factory, and what are your opinions about the way in which he is introduced to the firm?

3 Why do you think riding in the countryside gave so much pleasure to Colin?

4 When he is arrested, why doesn't Colin explain the truth about the bike?

5 What are Colin's feelings towards Bernard at the end?

6 What do you think of Colin? Is he a fool? Is he really as criminal as Bernard?

The Ragman's Daughter

7 What impressions do you get of Tony in the first few pages before he meets Doris? Why does he steal?

8 Doris is good-looking; is there anything else about her which attracts Tony on their first two meetings?

9 Why did Doris and Tony so enjoy their various robberies?

10 After Doris had been coming to Tony's house for a while, someone asked him when they were going to get married. Why hadn't they considered marriage?

11 What led to their being caught on the last raid in the shoe-shop?

12 What does Tony mean when he says (page 30): "All she wanted, I sometimes thought, was a world with kicks but I didn't fancy being for long at the mercy of a world in pit boots"? Are Doris and Tony very similar or are there any big differences between them?

13 Why do you think Doris married the garage mechanic? Had she lost all memory of Tony?

14 How does Tony behave when he first comes out of jail?

15 What is Tony really like by the end of the story? Has he changed since his first meeting with Doris?

Noah's Ark

16 Colin was easily distracted from the lesson. Do you think this was normal for him?

17 Why did Colin feel guilty about going to the fair?

18 Do you get the impression from the story that the author is sympathetic or critical towards the behaviour of the boys? What helps you make up your mind?

19 What picture do you get of the everyday life of Colin and Bert?

20 Consider the last sentence carefully. Why do you think Colin was so keen on the singing?

21 Look back over the story, and describe the differences between the characters of the two boys.

The Firebug

22 What is it that first gives the young boy such an interest in fires?

23 What is this boy's childhood like? Consider his house, his mother's way of looking after him, what we know about his father, and our general impression of the family life.

24 Is the boy stupid, or are there any signs of his being reasonably clever? Is he generally criminal, or have we any evidence that in certain ways he is likely to be law-abiding?

25 How is he affected by his final success in lighting the fire in the woods?

26 What clue about the story is given by the last sentence?

On Saturday Afternoon

27 We only know about his family through the boy's own description. What picture do we get of his family life?

28 Does the boy fully realise what the man is planning to do?

29 After the attempted hanging, the boy says that the man had "a normal frightened look in his eyes now" (page 74). Why "normal"?

Uncle Ernest

30 What sort of person do we think Ernest is at the start of the story, by the sixth paragraph?

31 Did people take much notice of him?

32 What was the result of the First World War on Ernest? Why didn't he have a pension after it?

33 What is his life like now?

34 What led Ernest to speak to the girls in the first place?

35 Why does he buy food for them day after day?

36 How does their behaviour towards him change?

37 Did his buying food and presents harm the two girls at all?

38 Did Ernest's attitude to *them* change?

39 Do you consider the customers were right to inform the police?

40 Why did the policemen say he'd known Ernest for years?

41 Describe what you think the effect of the policemen's warning will be on Ernest.

The Fishing-boat Picture

42 Why docs Harry actually marry Kathy?

43 What difference does marriage make to him?

44 What really started the final row which led to Kathy's leaving?

45 How was Harry changed by Kathy's departure?

46 When Kathy called that Friday night after so many years, did she and Harry behave as you would expect them to?

47 Why do you think Kathy visited him so regularly and for so long after that?

48 At the funeral, what surprised Harry, and why was it such a surprise?

49 Looking back over the story, do you think Harry was to *blame* for Kathy's unhappiness? Is it possible to explain why this marriage was such a failure?

The Decline and Fall of Frankie Buller

50 What kind of a person does the story-teller seem to have become by the start of the story?

51 How would doctors have described Frankie before the war?

52 What did the adults in the town think of him?

53 How did Frankie keep his authority over the boys?

54 How does the story-teller feel towards Frankie when they meet again after the ten years' break?

55 What does the story-teller mean when he says that "the conscientious-scientific-methodical probers . . . had no power in the long run really to *harm* such minds"?

56 Why did this final meeting with Frankie so move the story-teller?

The Nottingham Scene

A sequence of photographs by Andrew Whittuck

These photographs are not an attempt to illustrate the stories with pictures that exactly fit the key moments. They are instead the record of a photographer looking at Nottingham after reading the stories. They are included to help the reader picture the background of the stories, a background which is so important that it becomes almost one of the characters.

Coca-Cola
CAFÉ
DRINK
Coca-Cola
SNACKS

CAFE
SNACKS LUNCHES
TEAS COFFEE
106
PLAYER'S
SNACKS